THE ADVENTURES OF Huckleberry Finn

CAMPFIRE®

KALYANI NAVYUG MEDIA PVT LTD

THE ADVENTURES OF Huckleberry Finn

Wordsmith	:	**Roland Mann**
Illustrator	:	**Naresh Kumar**
Colorist	:	**Prince Varghese**
Letterer	:	**Bhavnath Chaudhary**
Editors	:	**Mark Jones**
		Divya Dubey
Designer	:	**Era Chawla**
Cover Artists	:	**Naresh Kumar**
		Vijay Sharma

CAMPFIRE®

www.campfire.co.in

Mission Statement

To entertain and educate young minds by creating unique illustrated books that recount stories of human values, arouse curiosity in the world around us, and inspire with tales of great deeds of unforgettable people.

Published by Kalyani Navyug Media Pvt Ltd
101 C, Shiv House, Hari Nagar Ashram
New Delhi 110014
India

ISBN: 978-93-80028-35-4

Printed in India

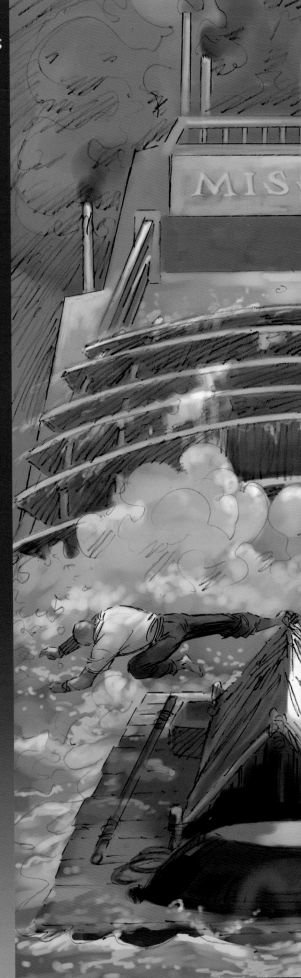

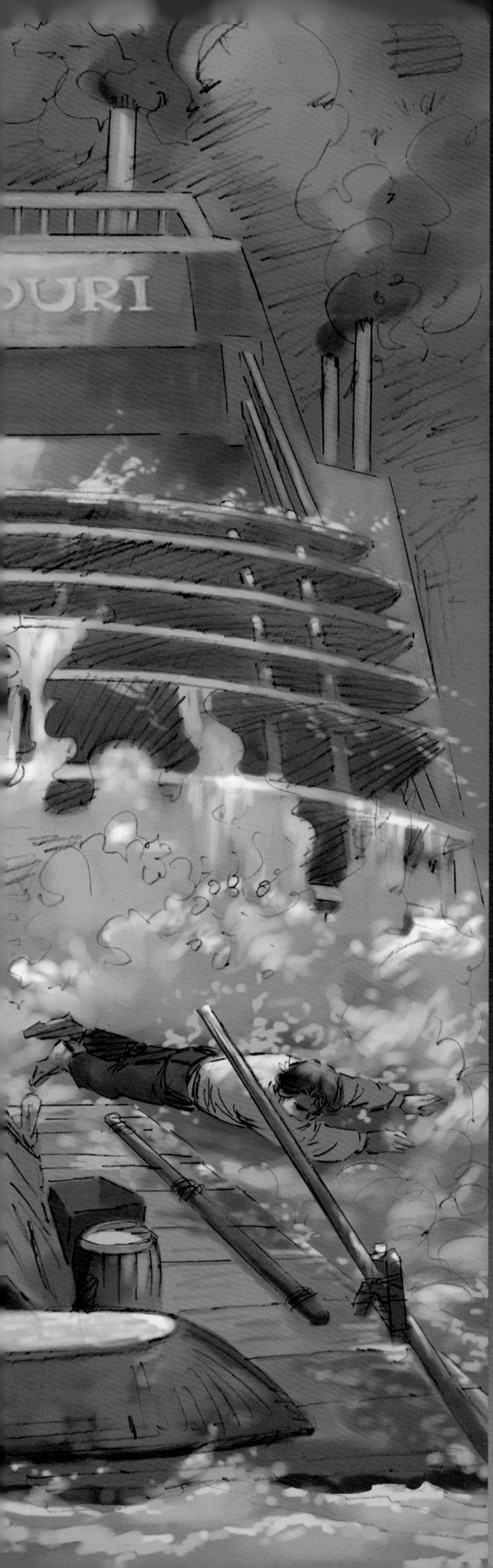
OURI

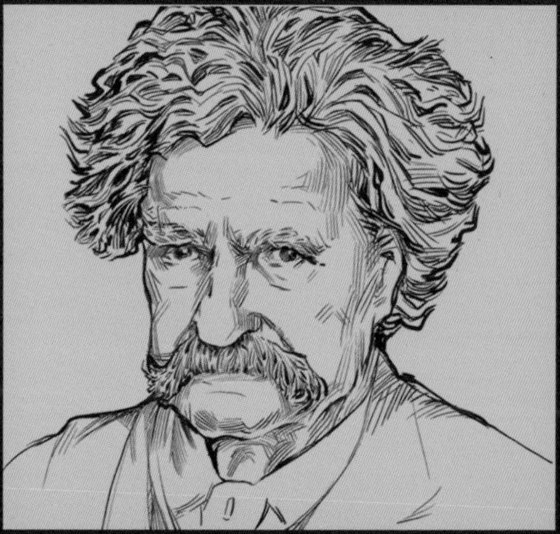

About The Author

Samuel Langhorne Clemens, known to most as Mark Twain, has been hailed by many as the father of American Literature. His two most famous works, *The Adventures of Tom Sawyer* (1876) and *The Adventures of Huckleberry Finn* (1884), are considered two of the greatest American novels of all time.

Twain was born in Florida, Missouri on November 30th, 1835. He grew up in the town of Hannibal on the Mississippi River, which would eventually serve as the basis for the place where Tom Sawyer and Huckleberry Finn would live.

Twain tried turning his hand to many different professions throughout his life, but continued writing all the while. His first job was as a printer's apprentice and, during this time, he met a famous steamboat captain who convinced him to become a pilot. After two years of training, he acquired his licence and began traversing the mighty Mississippi as the pilot of a steamboat. It was a dangerous and lucrative form of employment.

Twain grew up in Missouri at a time when it was a slave state. After the American Civil War broke out, he became a strong supporter of emancipation, and staunchly believed that the slave trade should be abolished.

Though he began as a comic writer, the tribulations he faced in his personal life perhaps served to turn him into a serious, even pessimistic, writer in his later years. He lost his wife and two daughters, and his ill-fated life never really allowed him to recover. Twain passed away in 1910, but he is still one of the best-loved writers around the world.

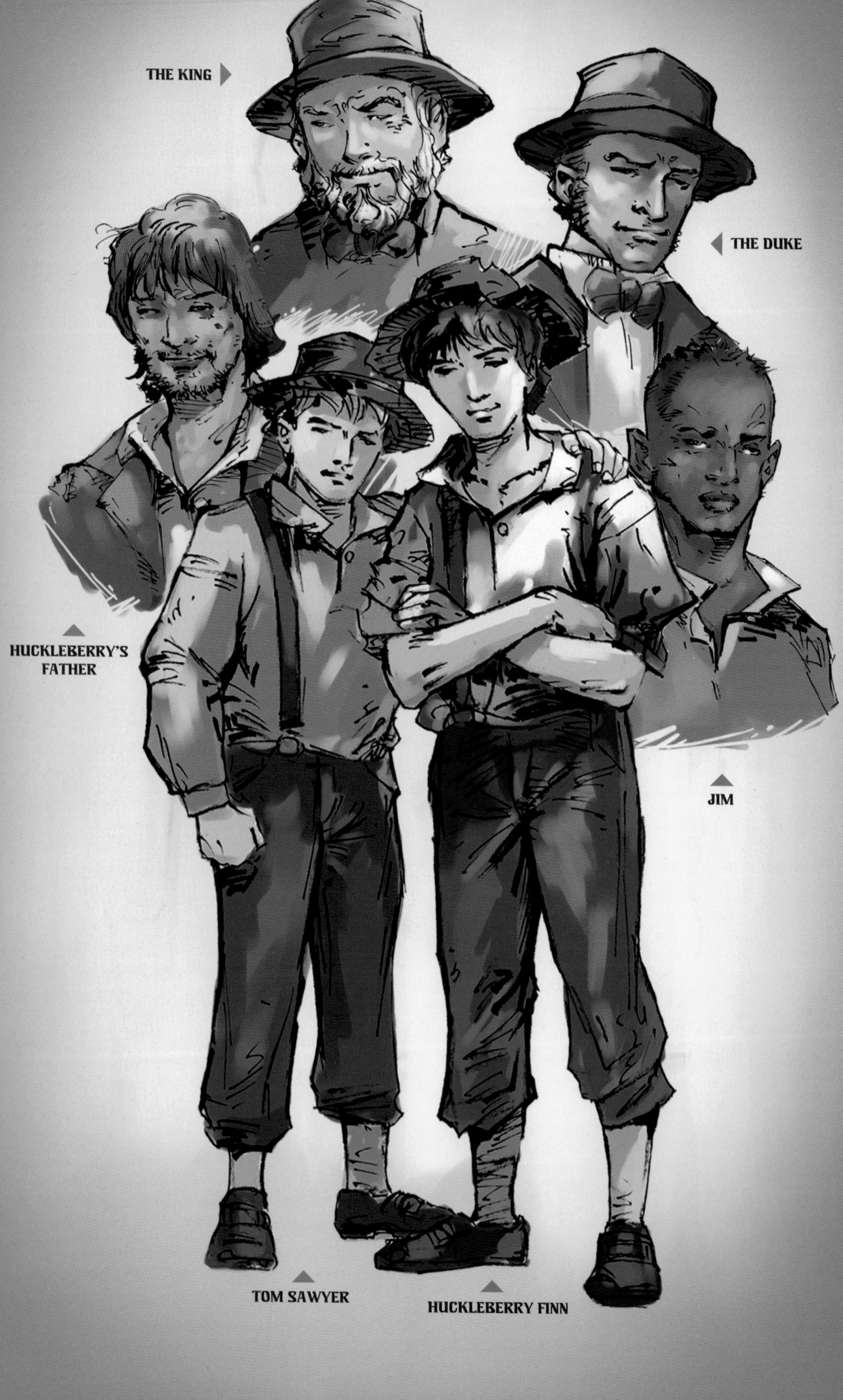
THE KING
THE DUKE
HUCKLEBERRY'S FATHER
JIM
TOM SAWYER
HUCKLEBERRY FINN

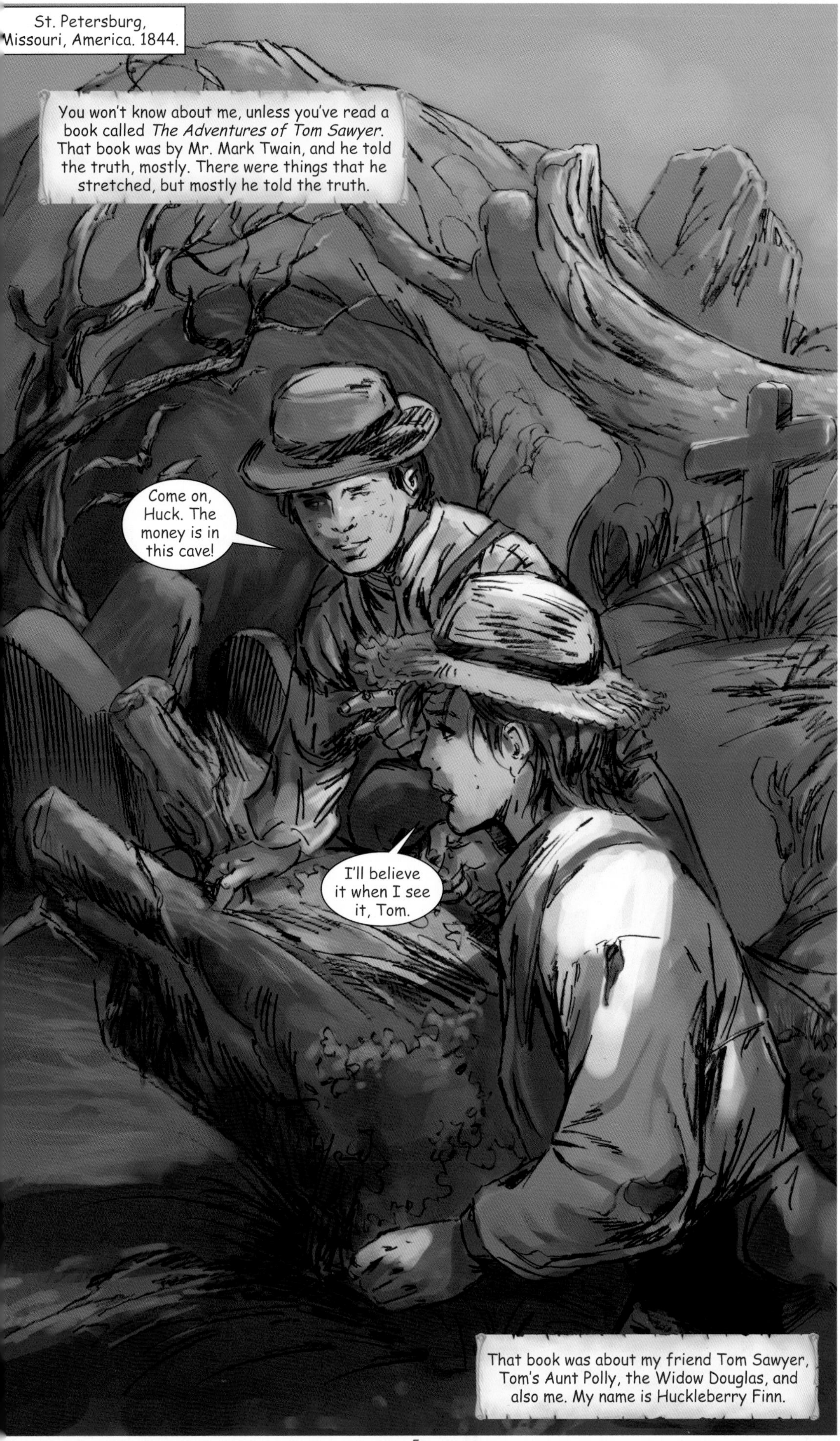
St. Petersburg, Missouri, America. 1844.
You won't know about me, unless you've read a book called *The Adventures of Tom Sawyer*. That book was by Mr. Mark Twain, and he told the truth, mostly. There were things that he stretched, but mostly he told the truth.
Come on, Huck. The money is in this cave!
I'll believe it when I see it, Tom.
That book was about my friend Tom Sawyer, Tom's Aunt Polly, the Widow Douglas, and also me. My name is Huckleberry Finn.

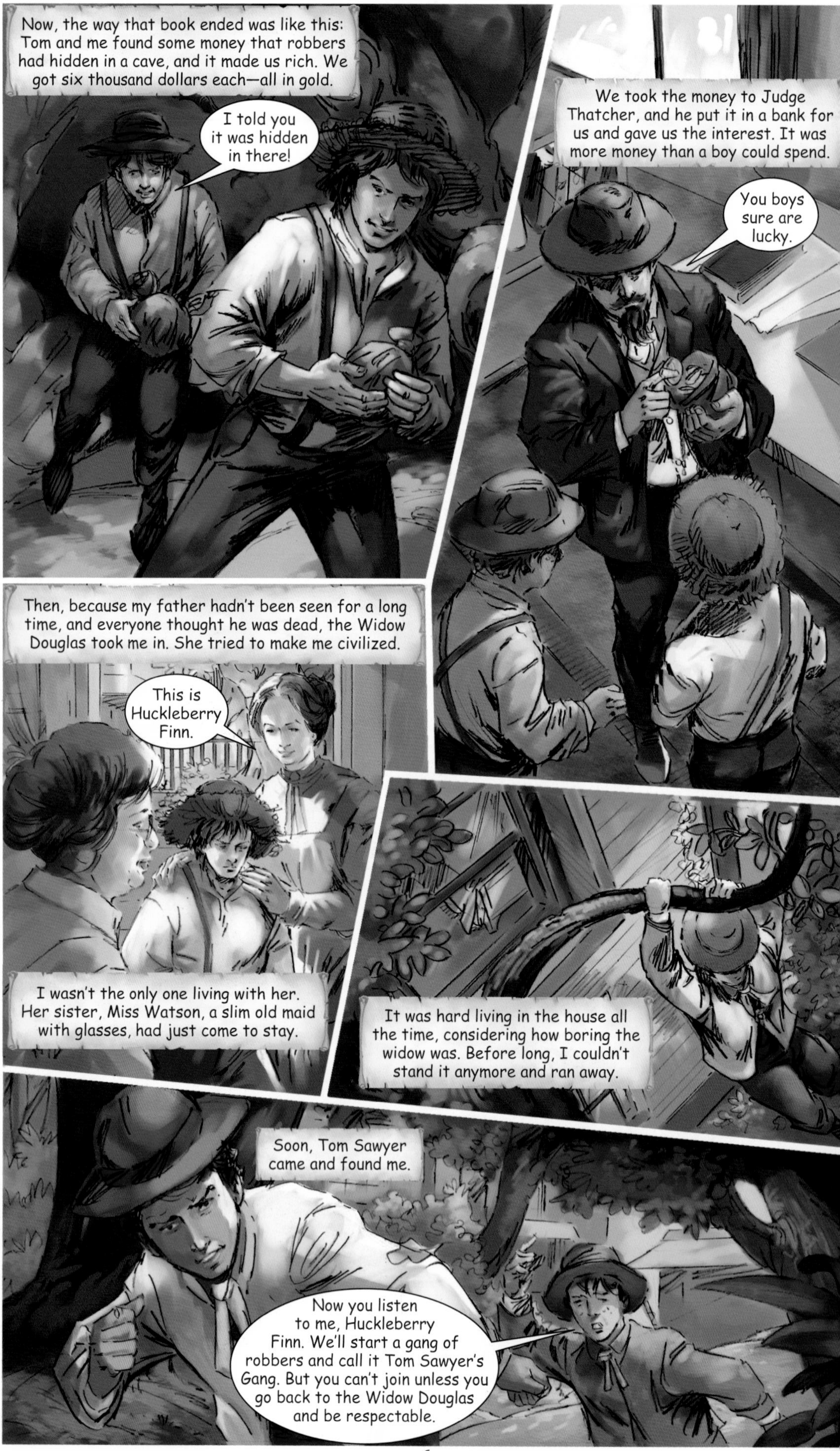
Now, the way that book ended was like this: Tom and me found some money that robbers had hidden in a cave, and it made us rich. We got six thousand dollars each—all in gold.
I told you it was hidden in there!
We took the money to Judge Thatcher, and he put it in a bank for us and gave us the interest. It was more money than a boy could spend.
You boys sure are lucky.
Then, because my father hadn't been seen for a long time, and everyone thought he was dead, the Widow Douglas took me in. She tried to make me civilized.
This is Huckleberry Finn.
I wasn't the only one living with her. Her sister, Miss Watson, a slim old maid with glasses, had just come to stay.
It was hard living in the house all the time, considering how boring the widow was. Before long, I couldn't stand it anymore and ran away.
Soon, Tom Sawyer came and found me.
Now you listen to me, Huckleberry Finn. We'll start a gang of robbers and call it Tom Sawyer's Gang. But you can't join unless you go back to the Widow Douglas and be respectable.

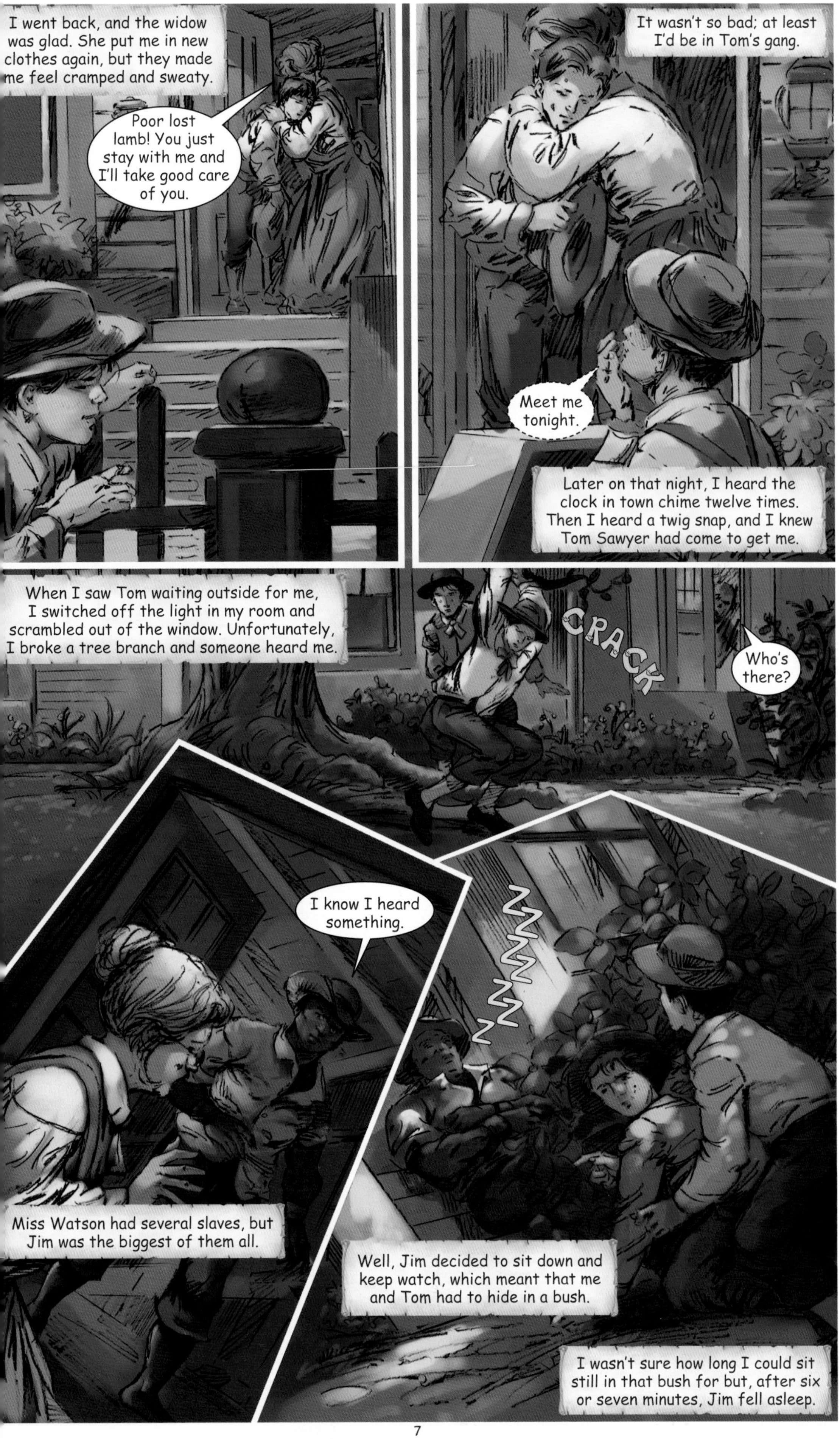
I went back, and the widow was glad. She put me in new clothes again, but they made me feel cramped and sweaty.
Poor lost lamb! You just stay with me and I'll take good care of you.
It wasn't so bad; at least I'd be in Tom's gang.
Meet me tonight.
Later on that night, I heard the clock in town chime twelve times. Then I heard a twig snap, and I knew Tom Sawyer had come to get me.
When I saw Tom waiting outside for me, I switched off the light in my room and scrambled out of the window. Unfortunately, I broke a tree branch and someone heard me.
CRACK
Who's there?
I know I heard something.
Miss Watson had several slaves, but Jim was the biggest of them all.
ZZZZZ
Well, Jim decided to sit down and keep watch, which meant that me and Tom had to hide in a bush.
I wasn't sure how long I could sit still in that bush for but, after six or seven minutes, Jim fell asleep.

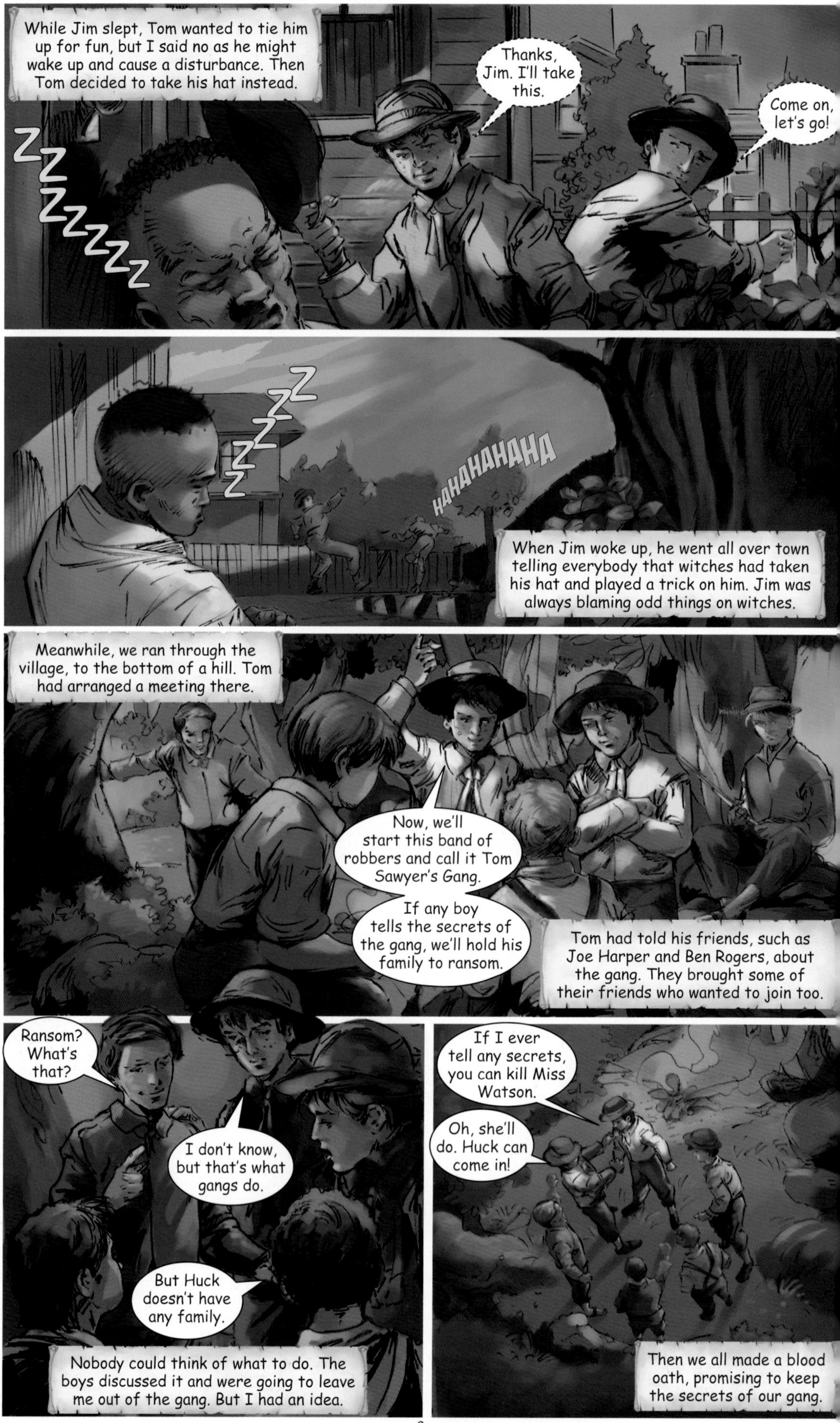

While Jim slept, Tom wanted to tie him up for fun, but I said no as he might wake up and cause a disturbance. Then Tom decided to take his hat instead.
ZZZZZZZ
Thanks, Jim. I'll take this.
Come on, let's go!
ZZZZZ
HAHAHAHAHA
When Jim woke up, he went all over town telling everybody that witches had taken his hat and played a trick on him. Jim was always blaming odd things on witches.
Meanwhile, we ran through the village, to the bottom of a hill. Tom had arranged a meeting there.
Now, we'll start this band of robbers and call it Tom Sawyer's Gang.
If any boy tells the secrets of the gang, we'll hold his family to ransom.
Tom had told his friends, such as Joe Harper and Ben Rogers, about the gang. They brought some of their friends who wanted to join too.
Ransom? What's that?
I don't know, but that's what gangs do.
But Huck doesn't have any family.
Nobody could think of what to do. The boys discussed it and were going to leave me out of the gang. But I had an idea.
If I ever tell any secrets, you can kill Miss Watson.
Oh, she'll do. Huck can come in!
Then we all made a blood oath, promising to keep the secrets of our gang.

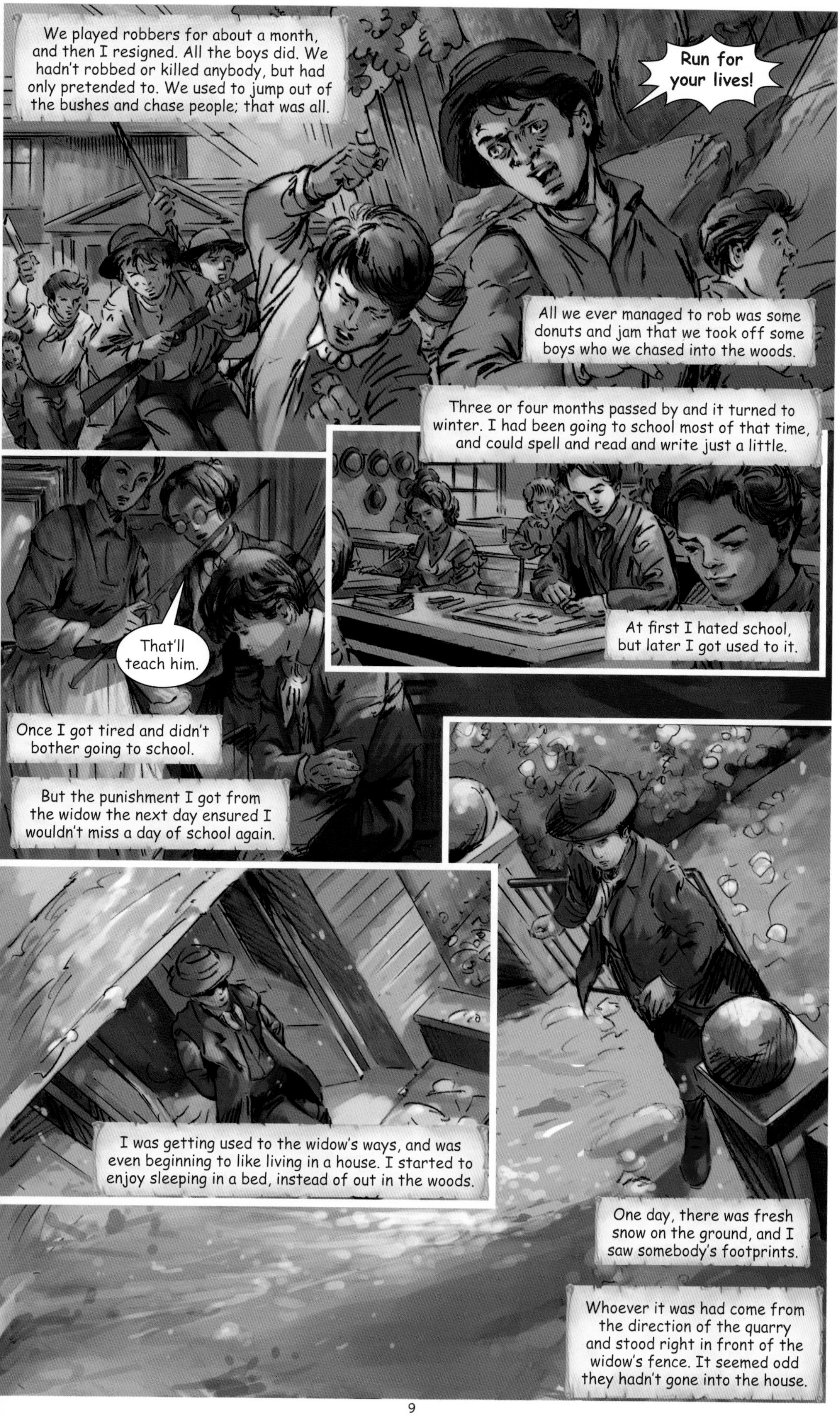
We played robbers for about a month, and then I resigned. All the boys did. We hadn't robbed or killed anybody, but had only pretended to. We used to jump out of the bushes and chase people; that was all.
Run for your lives!
All we ever managed to rob was some donuts and jam that we took off some boys who we chased into the woods.
Three or four months passed by and it turned to winter. I had been going to school most of that time, and could spell and read and write just a little.
At first I hated school, but later I got used to it.
That'll teach him.
Once I got tired and didn't bother going to school.
But the punishment I got from the widow the next day ensured I wouldn't miss a day of school again.
I was getting used to the widow's ways, and was even beginning to like living in a house. I started to enjoy sleeping in a bed, instead of out in the woods.
One day, there was fresh snow on the ground, and I saw somebody's footprints.
Whoever it was had come from the direction of the quarry and stood right in front of the widow's fence. It seemed odd they hadn't gone into the house.

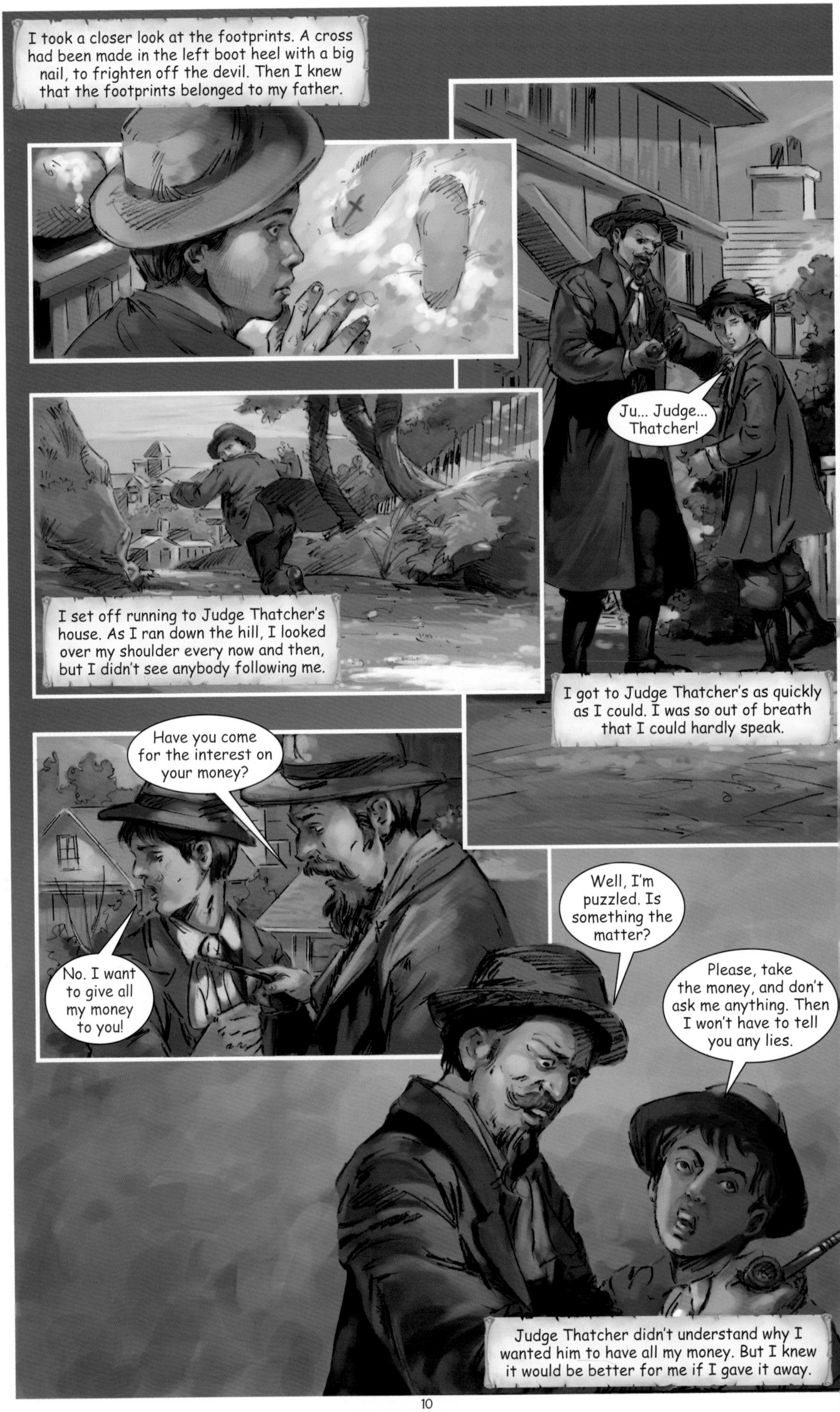

I took a closer look at the footprints. A cross had been made in the left boot heel with a big nail, to frighten off the devil. Then I knew that the footprints belonged to my father.
I set off running to Judge Thatcher's house. As I ran down the hill, I looked over my shoulder every now and then, but I didn't see anybody following me.
Ju... Judge... Thatcher!
I got to Judge Thatcher's as quickly as I could. I was so out of breath that I could hardly speak.
Have you come for the interest on your money?
No. I want to give all my money to you!
Well, I'm puzzled. Is something the matter?
Please, take the money, and don't ask me anything. Then I won't have to tell you any lies.
Judge Thatcher didn't understand why I wanted him to have all my money. But I knew it would be better for me if I gave it away.

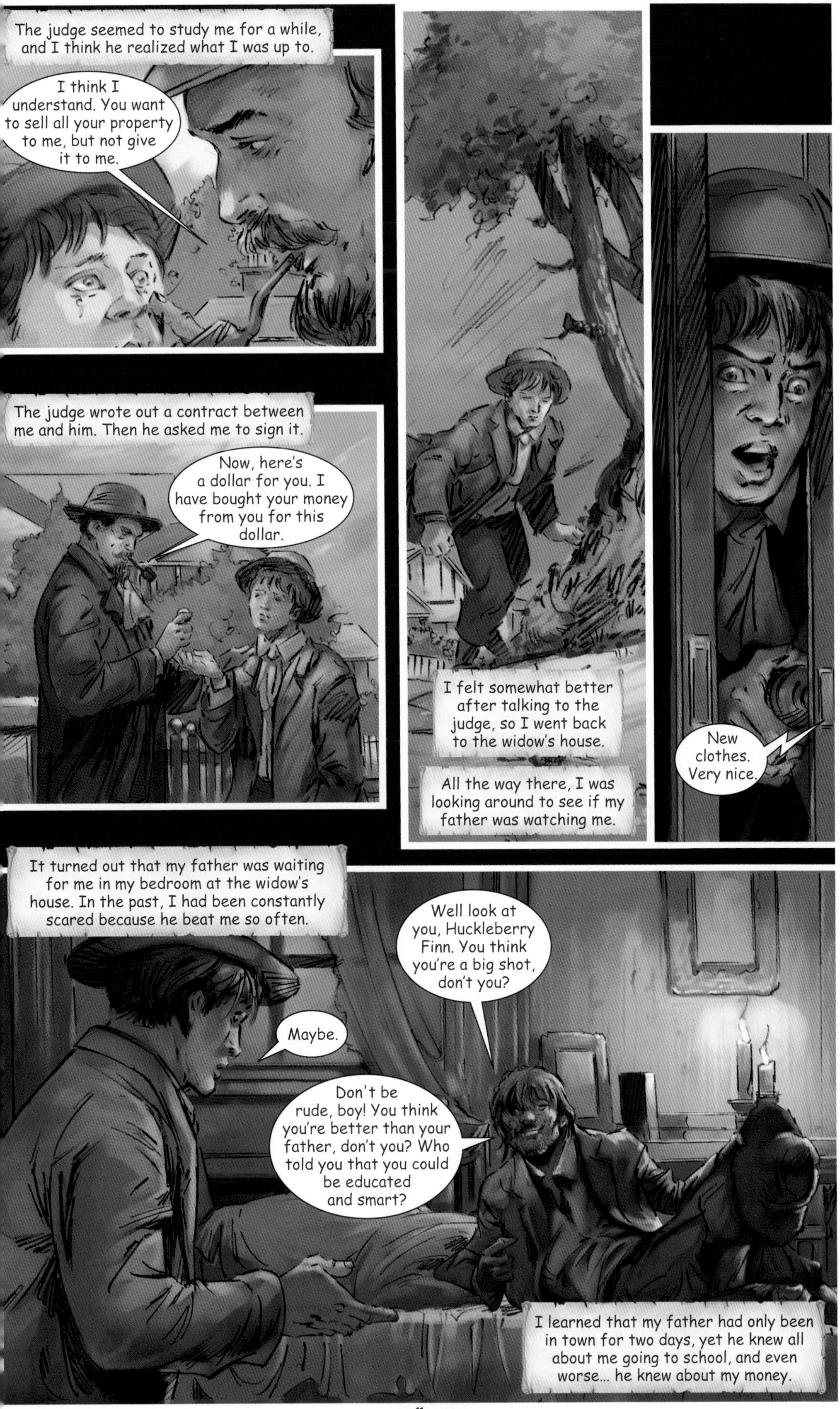
The judge seemed to study me for a while, and I think he realized what I was up to.
I think I understand. You want to sell all your property to me, but not give it to me.
The judge wrote out a contract between me and him. Then he asked me to sign it.
Now, here's a dollar for you. I have bought your money from you for this dollar.
I felt somewhat better after talking to the judge, so I went back to the widow's house.
All the way there, I was looking around to see if my father was watching me.
New clothes. Very nice.
It turned out that my father was waiting for me in my bedroom at the widow's house. In the past, I had been constantly scared because he beat me so often.
Well look at you, Huckleberry Finn. You think you're a big shot, don't you?
Maybe.
Don't be rude, boy! You think you're better than your father, don't you? Who told you that you could be educated and smart?
I learned that my father had only been in town for two days, yet he knew all about me going to school, and even worse... he knew about my money.

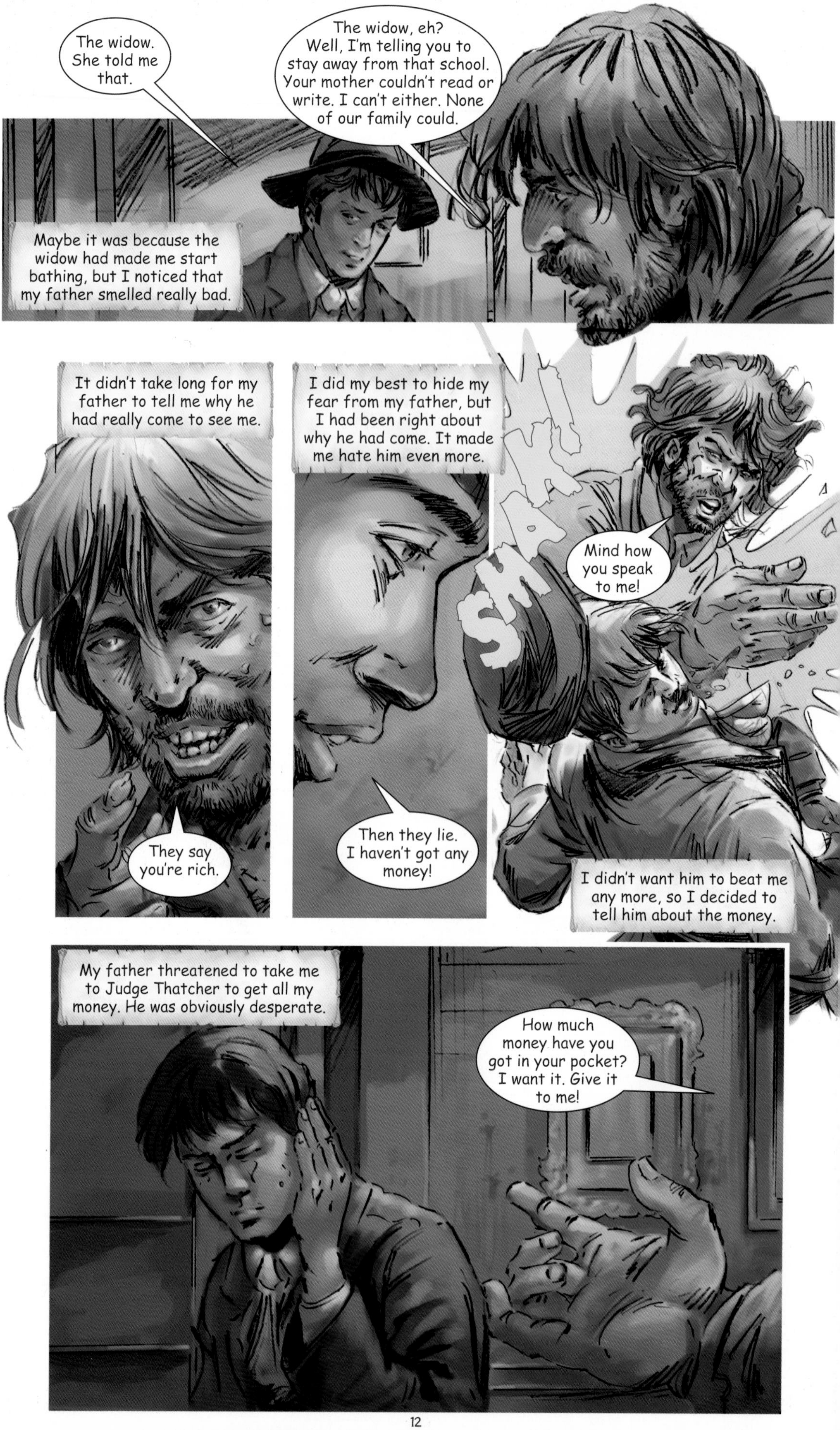
The widow. She told me that.
The widow, eh? Well, I'm telling you to stay away from that school. Your mother couldn't read or write. I can't either. None of our family could.
Maybe it was because the widow had made me start bathing, but I noticed that my father smelled really bad.
It didn't take long for my father to tell me why he had really come to see me.
They say you're rich.
I did my best to hide my fear from my father, but I had been right about why he had come. It made me hate him even more.
Then they lie. I haven't got any money!
Mind how you speak to me!
I didn't want him to beat me any more, so I decided to tell him about the money.
My father threatened to take me to Judge Thatcher to get all my money. He was obviously desperate.
How much money have you got in your pocket? I want it. Give it to me!

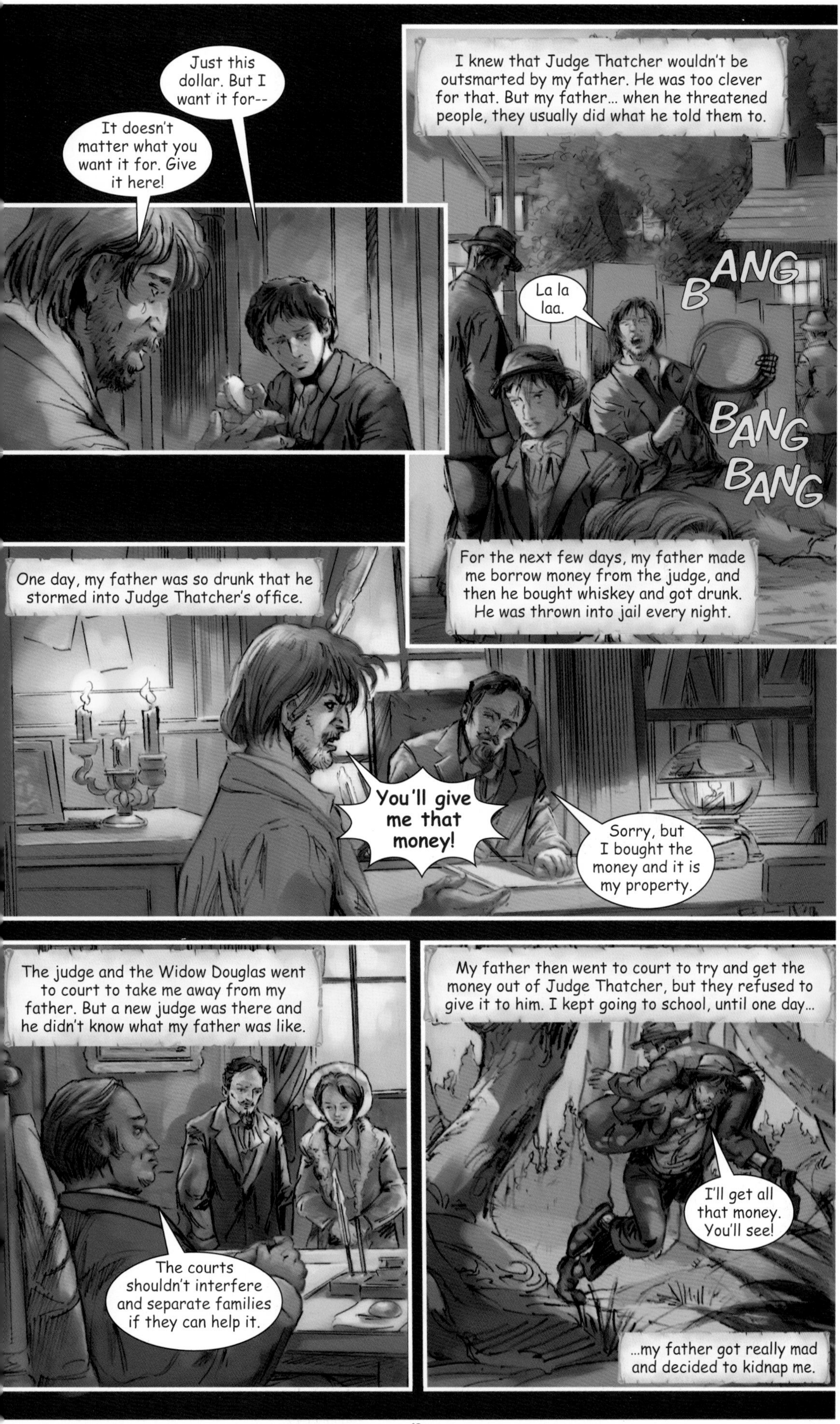
It doesn't matter what you want it for. Give it here!
Just this dollar. But I want it for--
I knew that Judge Thatcher wouldn't be outsmarted by my father. He was too clever for that. But my father... when he threatened people, they usually did what he told them to.
La la laa.
BANG
BANG
BANG
For the next few days, my father made me borrow money from the judge, and then he bought whiskey and got drunk. He was thrown into jail every night.
One day, my father was so drunk that he stormed into Judge Thatcher's office.
You'll give me that money!
Sorry, but I bought the money and it is my property.
The judge and the Widow Douglas went to court to take me away from my father. But a new judge was there and he didn't know what my father was like.
The courts shouldn't interfere and separate families if they can help it.
My father then went to court to try and get the money out of Judge Thatcher, but they refused to give it to him. I kept going to school, until one day...
I'll get all that money. You'll see!
...my father got really mad and decided to kidnap me.

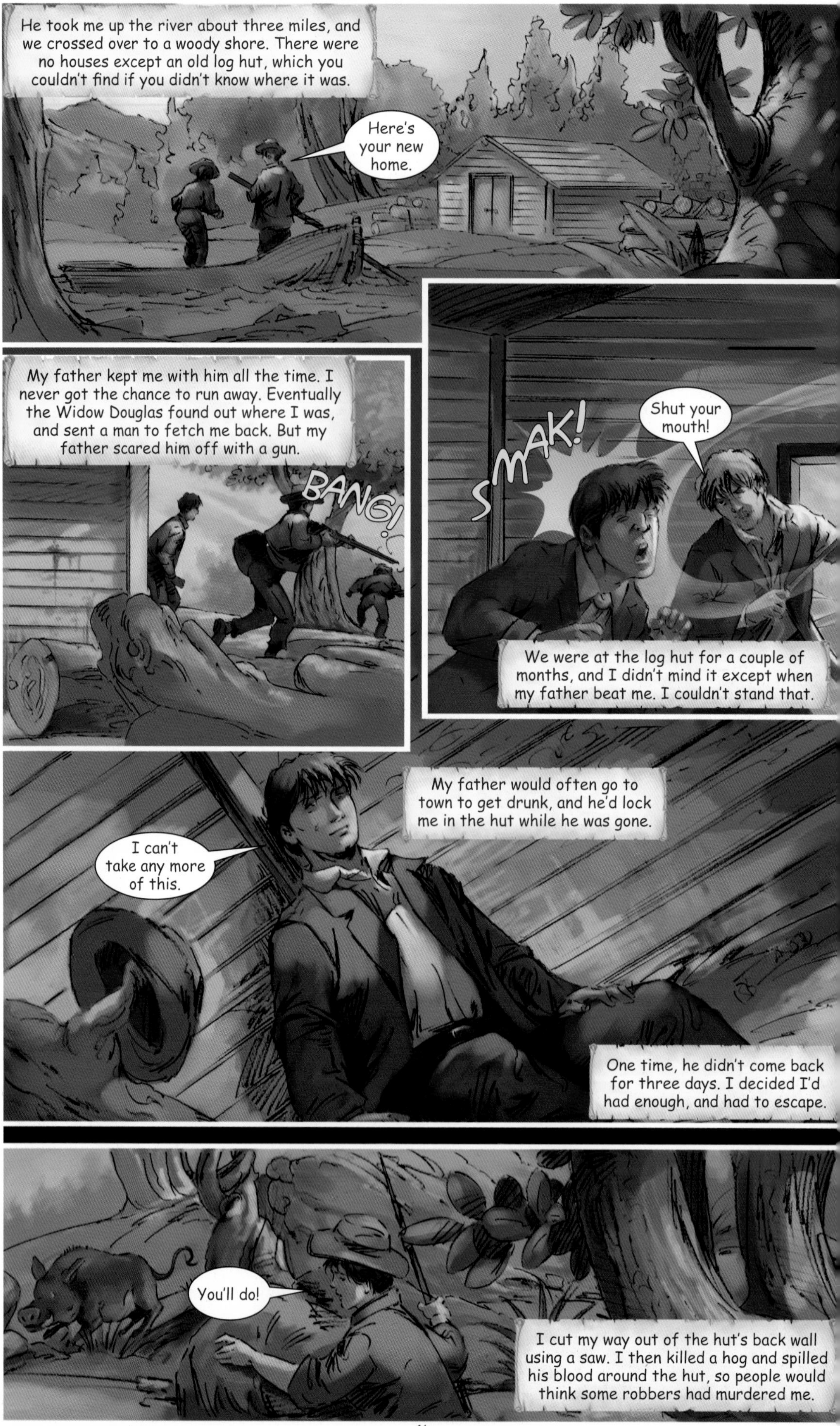
He took me up the river about three miles, and we crossed over to a woody shore. There were no houses except an old log hut, which you couldn't find if you didn't know where it was.
Here's your new home.
My father kept me with him all the time. I never got the chance to run away. Eventually the Widow Douglas found out where I was, and sent a man to fetch me back. But my father scared him off with a gun.
BANG!
SMAK!
Shut your mouth!
We were at the log hut for a couple of months, and I didn't mind it except when my father beat me. I couldn't stand that.
My father would often go to town to get drunk, and he'd lock me in the hut while he was gone.
I can't take any more of this.
One time, he didn't come back for three days. I decided I'd had enough, and had to escape.
You'll do!
I cut my way out of the hut's back wall using a saw. I then killed a hog and spilled his blood around the hut, so people would think some robbers had murdered me.

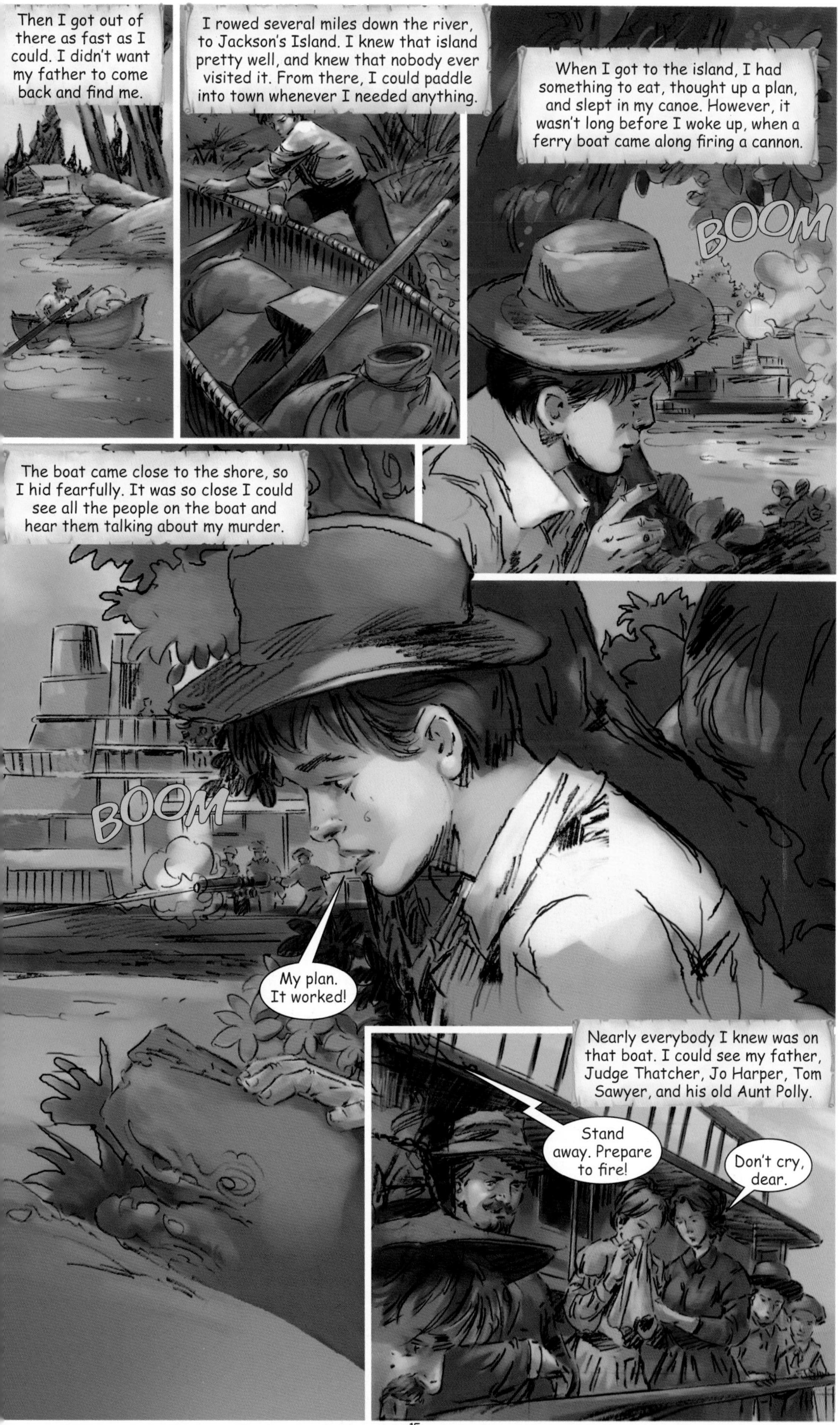
Then I got out of there as fast as I could. I didn't want my father to come back and find me.
I rowed several miles down the river, to Jackson's Island. I knew that island pretty well, and knew that nobody ever visited it. From there, I could paddle into town whenever I needed anything.
When I got to the island, I had something to eat, thought up a plan, and slept in my canoe. However, it wasn't long before I woke up, when a ferry boat came along firing a cannon.
BOOM
The boat came close to the shore, so I hid fearfully. It was so close I could see all the people on the boat and hear them talking about my murder.
BOOM
My plan. It worked!
Nearly everybody I knew was on that boat. I could see my father, Judge Thatcher, Jo Harper, Tom Sawyer, and his old Aunt Polly.
Stand away. Prepare to fire!
Don't cry, dear.

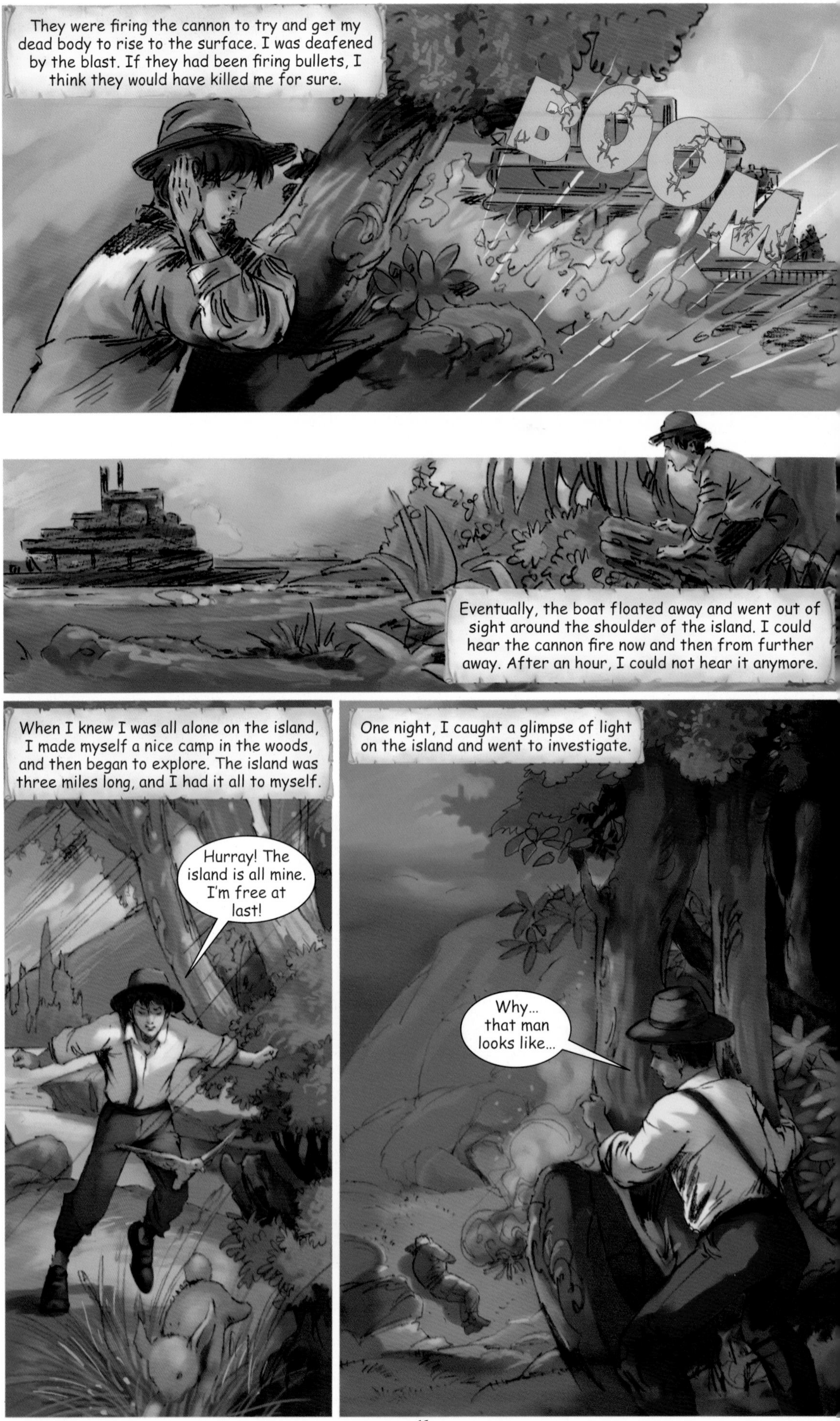
They were firing the cannon to try and get my dead body to rise to the surface. I was deafened by the blast. If they had been firing bullets, I think they would have killed me for sure.
BOOM
Eventually, the boat floated away and went out of sight around the shoulder of the island. I could hear the cannon fire now and then from further away. After an hour, I could not hear it anymore.
When I knew I was all alone on the island, I made myself a nice camp in the woods, and then began to explore. The island was three miles long, and I had it all to myself.
Hurray! The island is all mine. I'm free at last!
One night, I caught a glimpse of light on the island and went to investigate.
Why... that man looks like...

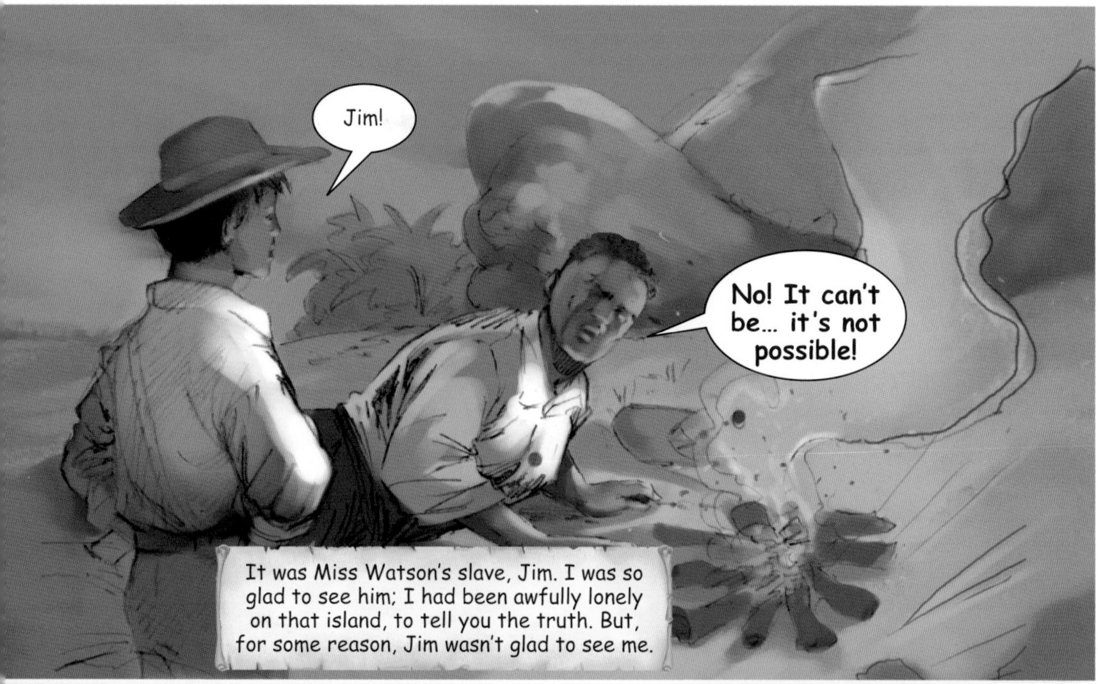
Jim!
No! It can't be... it's not possible!
It was Miss Watson's slave, Jim. I was so glad to see him; I had been awfully lonely on that island, to tell you the truth. But, for some reason, Jim wasn't glad to see me.

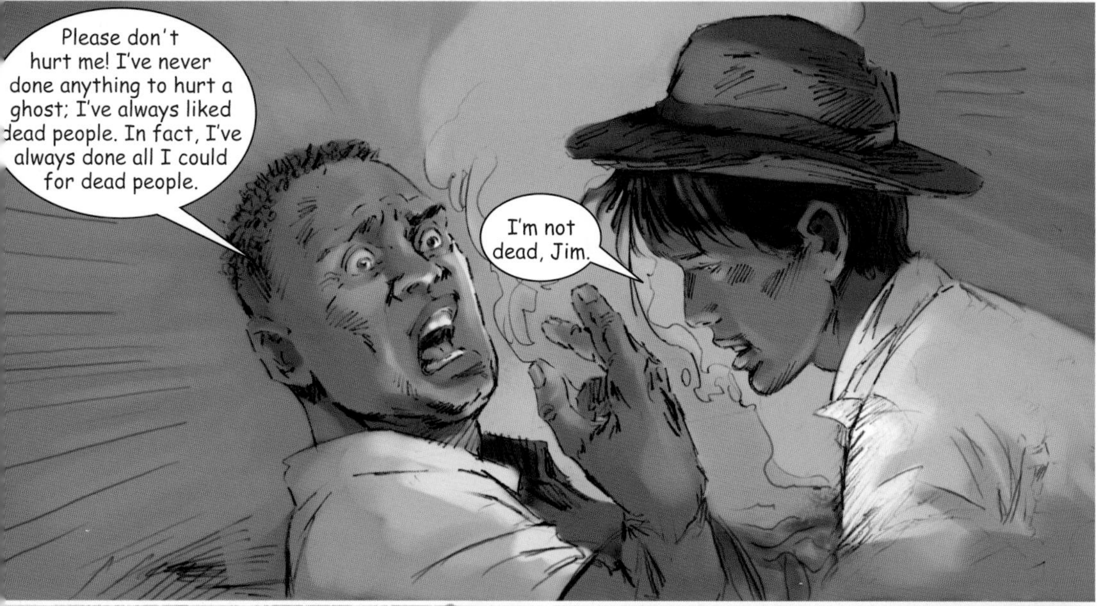
Please don't hurt me! I've never done anything to hurt a ghost; I've always liked dead people. In fact, I've always done all I could for dead people.
I'm not dead, Jim.

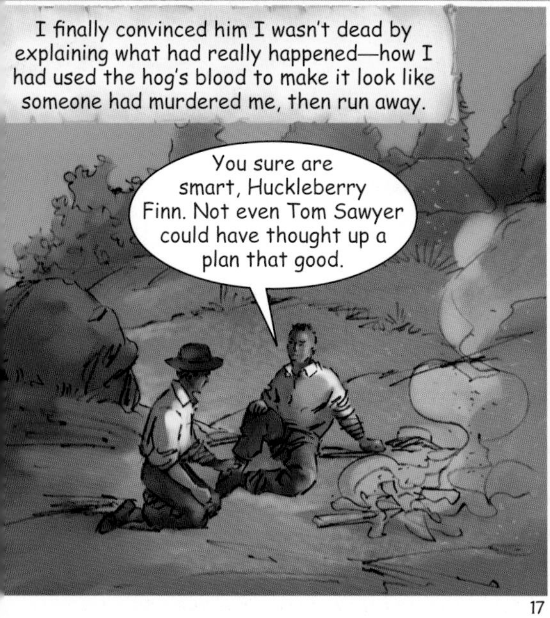
I finally convinced him I wasn't dead by explaining what had really happened—how I had used the hog's blood to make it look like someone had murdered me, then run away.
You sure are smart, Huckleberry Finn. Not even Tom Sawyer could have thought up a plan that good.

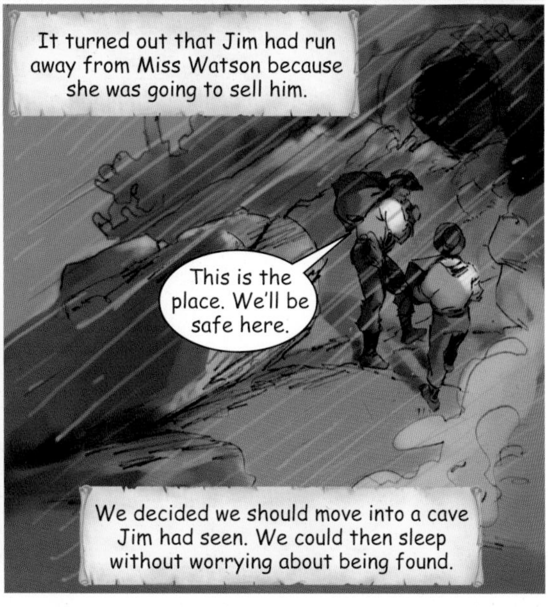
It turned out that Jim had run away from Miss Watson because she was going to sell him.
This is the place. We'll be safe here.
We decided we should move into a cave Jim had seen. We could then sleep without worrying about being found.

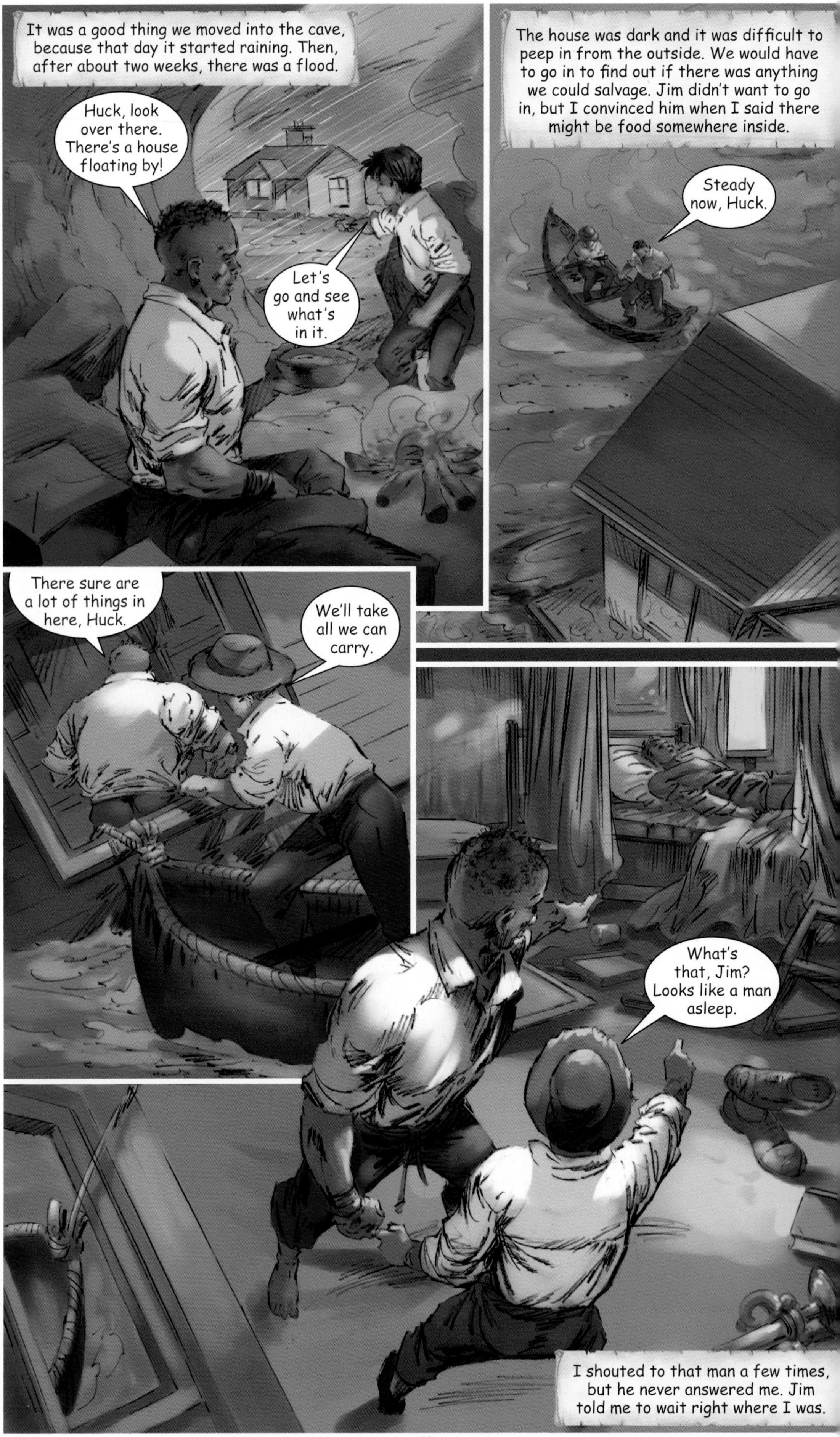

It was a good thing we moved into the cave, because that day it started raining. Then, after about two weeks, there was a flood.
Huck, look over there. There's a house floating by!
Let's go and see what's in it.
The house was dark and it was difficult to peep in from the outside. We would have to go in to find out if there was anything we could salvage. Jim didn't want to go in, but I convinced him when I said there might be food somewhere inside.
Steady now, Huck.
There sure are a lot of things in here, Huck.
We'll take all we can carry.
What's that, Jim? Looks like a man asleep.
I shouted to that man a few times, but he never answered me. Jim told me to wait right where I was.

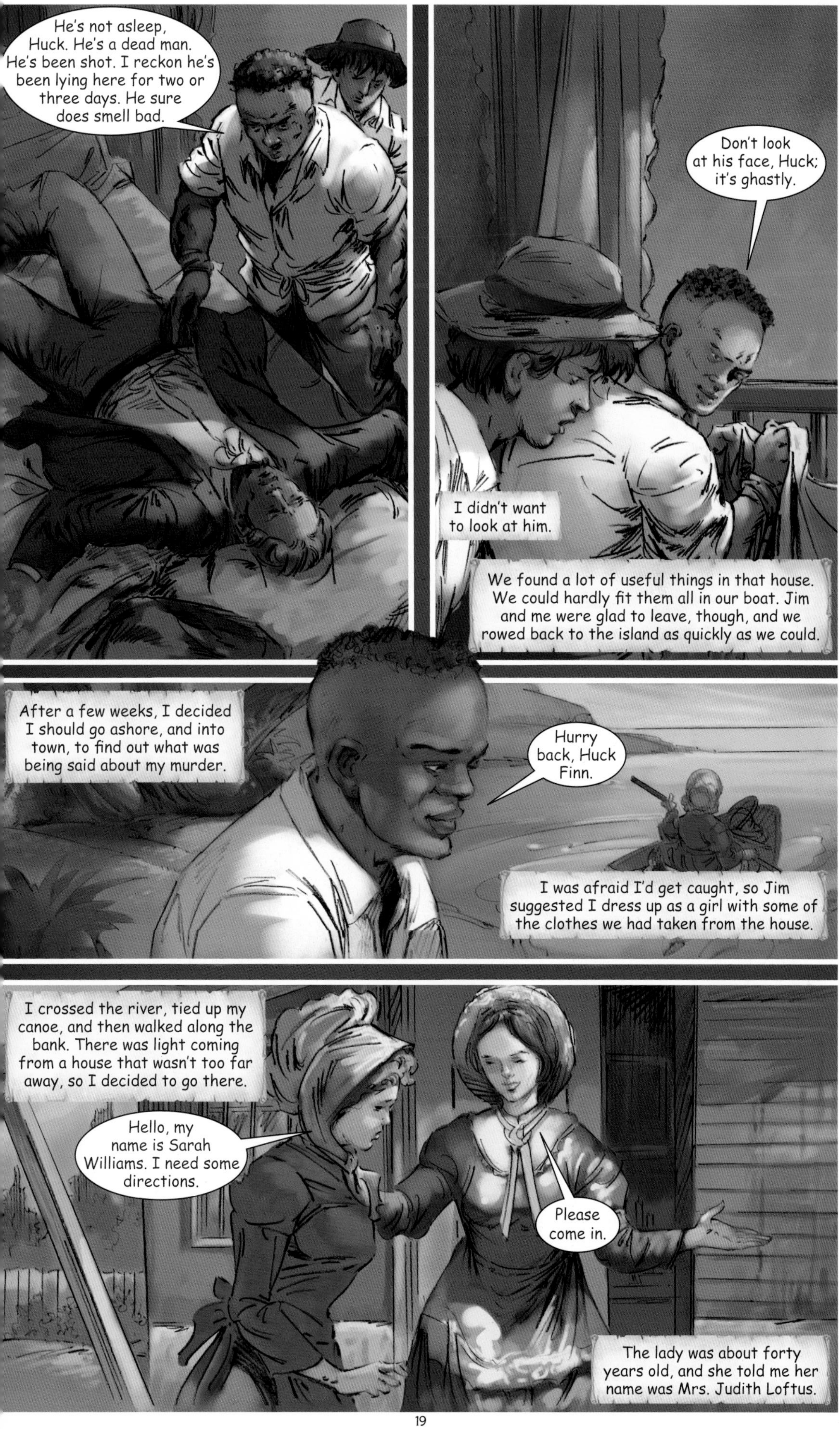
He's not asleep, Huck. He's a dead man. He's been shot. I reckon he's been lying here for two or three days. He sure does smell bad.
Don't look at his face, Huck; it's ghastly.
I didn't want to look at him.
We found a lot of useful things in that house. We could hardly fit them all in our boat. Jim and me were glad to leave, though, and we rowed back to the island as quickly as we could.
After a few weeks, I decided I should go ashore, and into town, to find out what was being said about my murder.
Hurry back, Huck Finn.
I was afraid I'd get caught, so Jim suggested I dress up as a girl with some of the clothes we had taken from the house.
I crossed the river, tied up my canoe, and then walked along the bank. There was light coming from a house that wasn't too far away, so I decided to go there.
Hello, my name is Sarah Williams. I need some directions.
Please come in.
The lady was about forty years old, and she told me her name was Mrs. Judith Loftus.

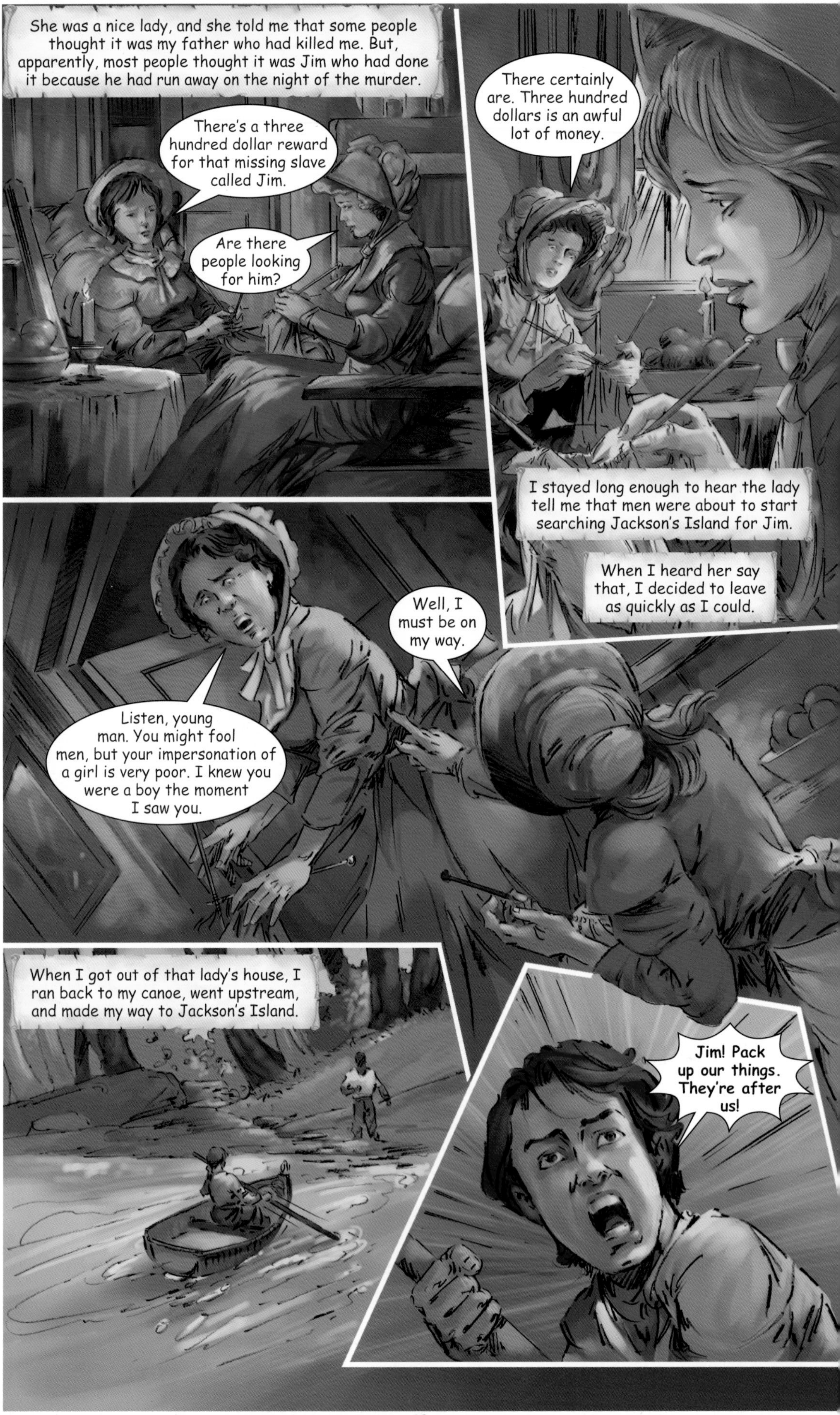
She was a nice lady, and she told me that some people thought it was my father who had killed me. But, apparently, most people thought it was Jim who had done it because he had run away on the night of the murder.
There's a three hundred dollar reward for that missing slave called Jim.
Are there people looking for him?
There certainly are. Three hundred dollars is an awful lot of money.
I stayed long enough to hear the lady tell me that men were about to start searching Jackson's Island for Jim.
When I heard her say that, I decided to leave as quickly as I could.
Well, I must be on my way.
Listen, young man. You might fool men, but your impersonation of a girl is very poor. I knew you were a boy the moment I saw you.
When I got out of that lady's house, I ran back to my canoe, went upstream, and made my way to Jackson's Island.
Jim! Pack up our things. They're after us!

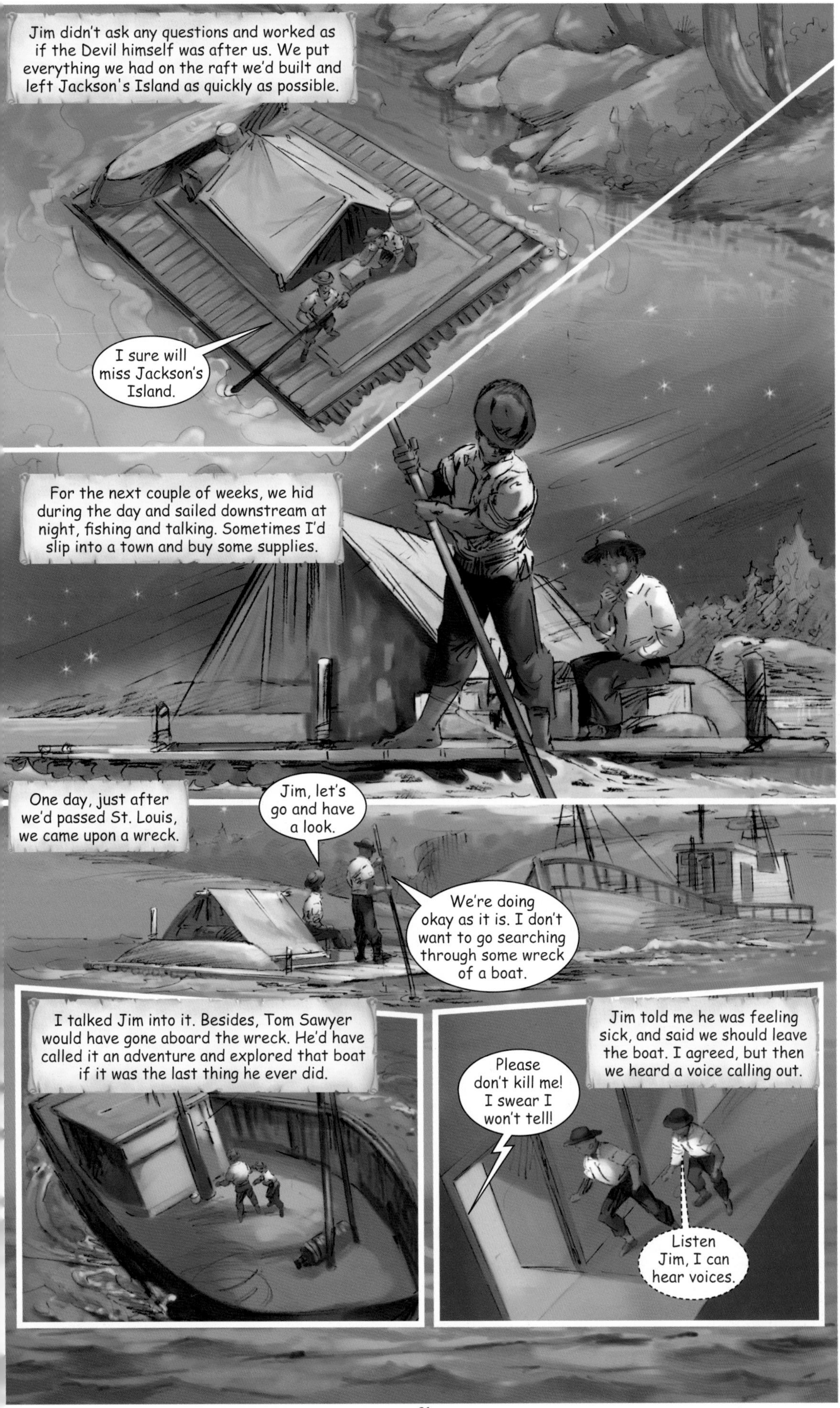
Jim didn't ask any questions and worked as if the Devil himself was after us. We put everything we had on the raft we'd built and left Jackson's Island as quickly as possible.
I sure will miss Jackson's Island.
For the next couple of weeks, we hid during the day and sailed downstream at night, fishing and talking. Sometimes I'd slip into a town and buy some supplies.
One day, just after we'd passed St. Louis, we came upon a wreck.
Jim, let's go and have a look.
We're doing okay as it is. I don't want to go searching through some wreck of a boat.
I talked Jim into it. Besides, Tom Sawyer would have gone aboard the wreck. He'd have called it an adventure and explored that boat if it was the last thing he ever did.
Jim told me he was feeling sick, and said we should leave the boat. I agreed, but then we heard a voice calling out.
Please don't kill me! I swear I won't tell!
Listen Jim, I can hear voices.

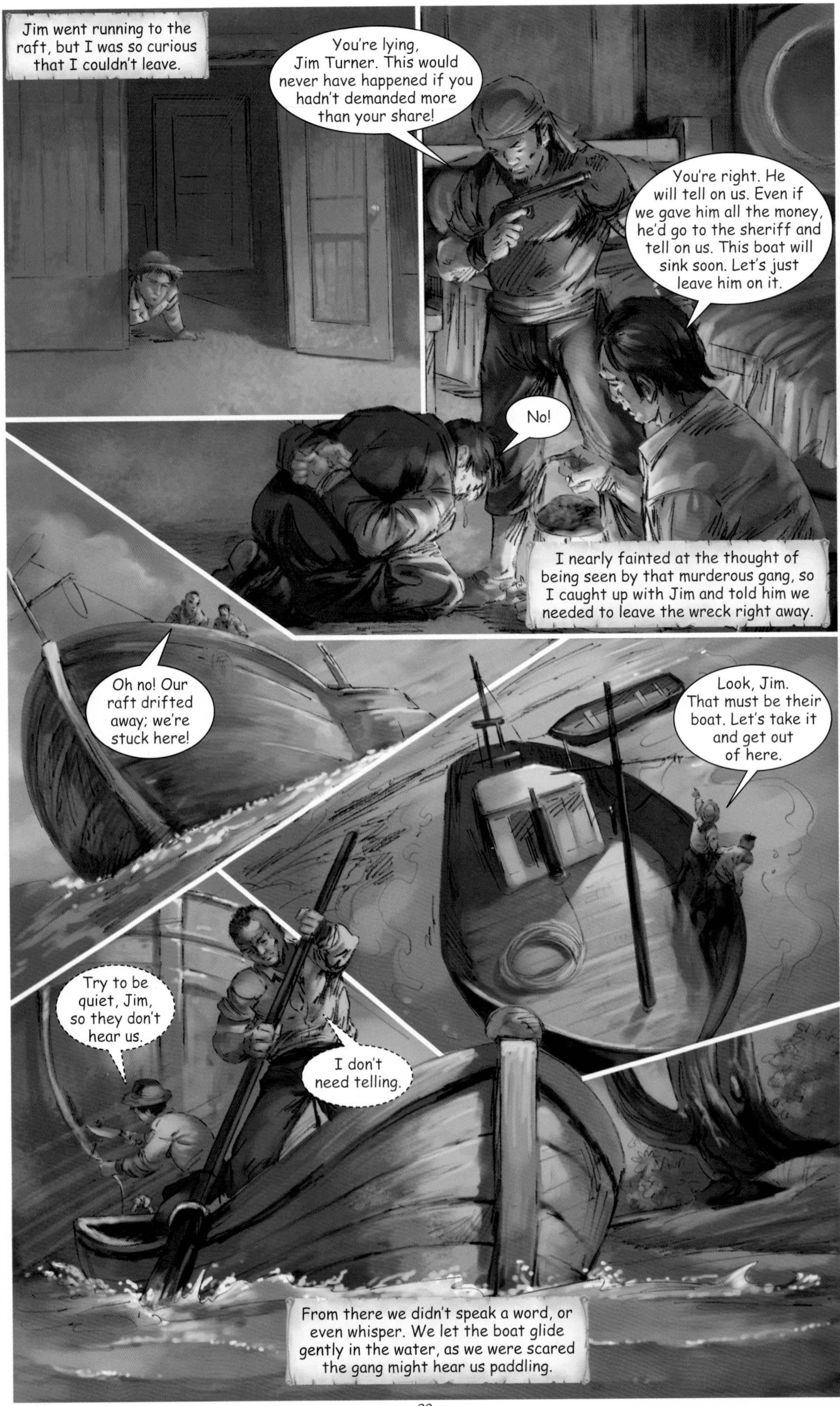

Jim went running to the raft, but I was so curious that I couldn't leave.
You're lying, Jim Turner. This would never have happened if you hadn't demanded more than your share!
You're right. He will tell on us. Even if we gave him all the money, he'd go to the sheriff and tell on us. This boat will sink soon. Let's just leave him on it.
No!
I nearly fainted at the thought of being seen by that murderous gang, so I caught up with Jim and told him we needed to leave the wreck right away.
Oh no! Our raft drifted away; we're stuck here!
Look, Jim. That must be their boat. Let's take it and get out of here.
Try to be quiet, Jim, so they don't hear us.
I don't need telling.
From there we didn't speak a word, or even whisper. We let the boat glide gently in the water, as we were scared the gang might hear us paddling.

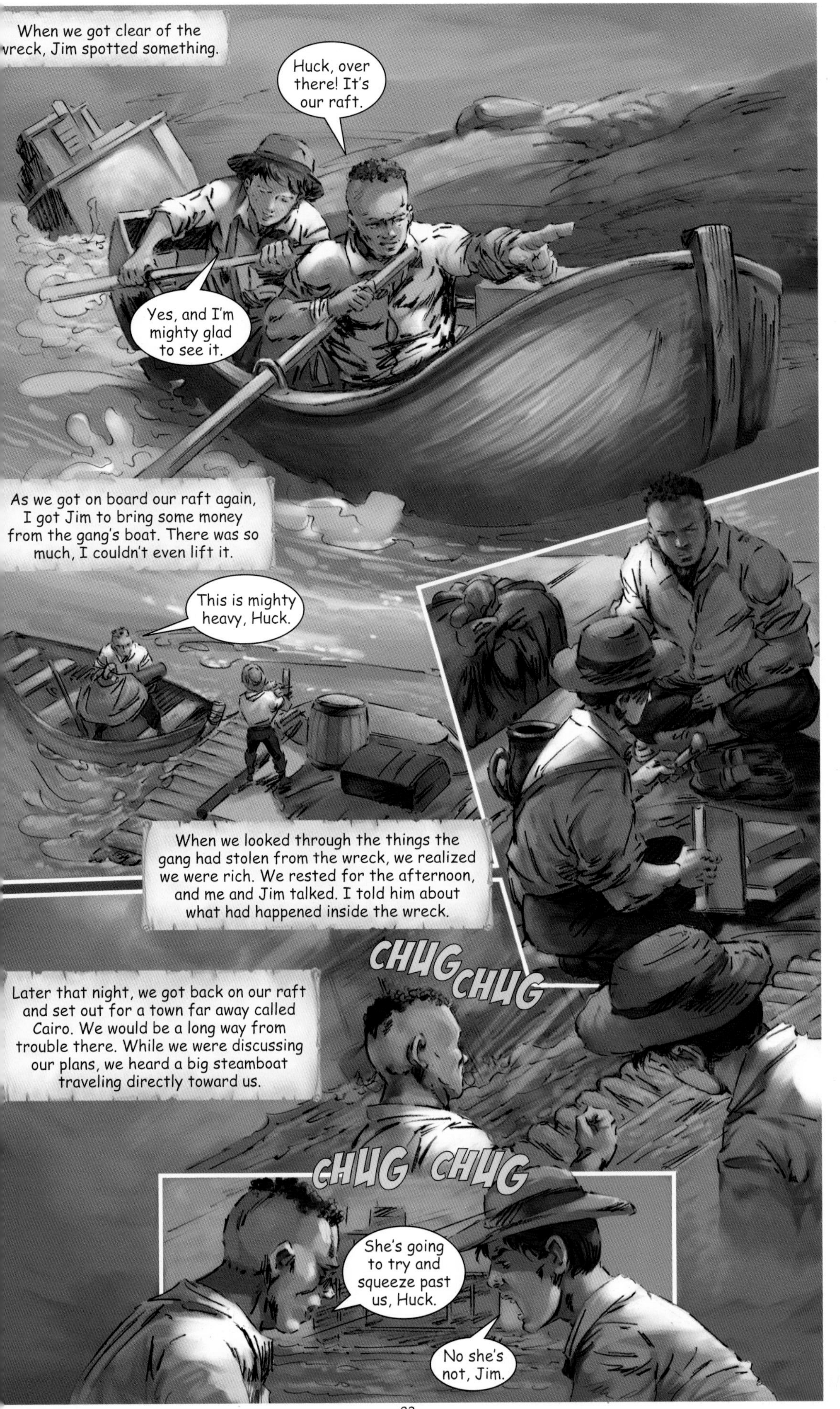

When we got clear of the wreck, Jim spotted something.
Huck, over there! It's our raft.
Yes, and I'm mighty glad to see it.
As we got on board our raft again, I got Jim to bring some money from the gang's boat. There was so much, I couldn't even lift it.
This is mighty heavy, Huck.
When we looked through the things the gang had stolen from the wreck, we realized we were rich. We rested for the afternoon, and me and Jim talked. I told him about what had happened inside the wreck.
Later that night, we got back on our raft and set out for a town far away called Cairo. We would be a long way from trouble there. While we were discussing our plans, we heard a big steamboat traveling directly toward us.
CHUG CHUG
CHUG CHUG
She's going to try and squeeze past us, Huck.
No she's not, Jim.

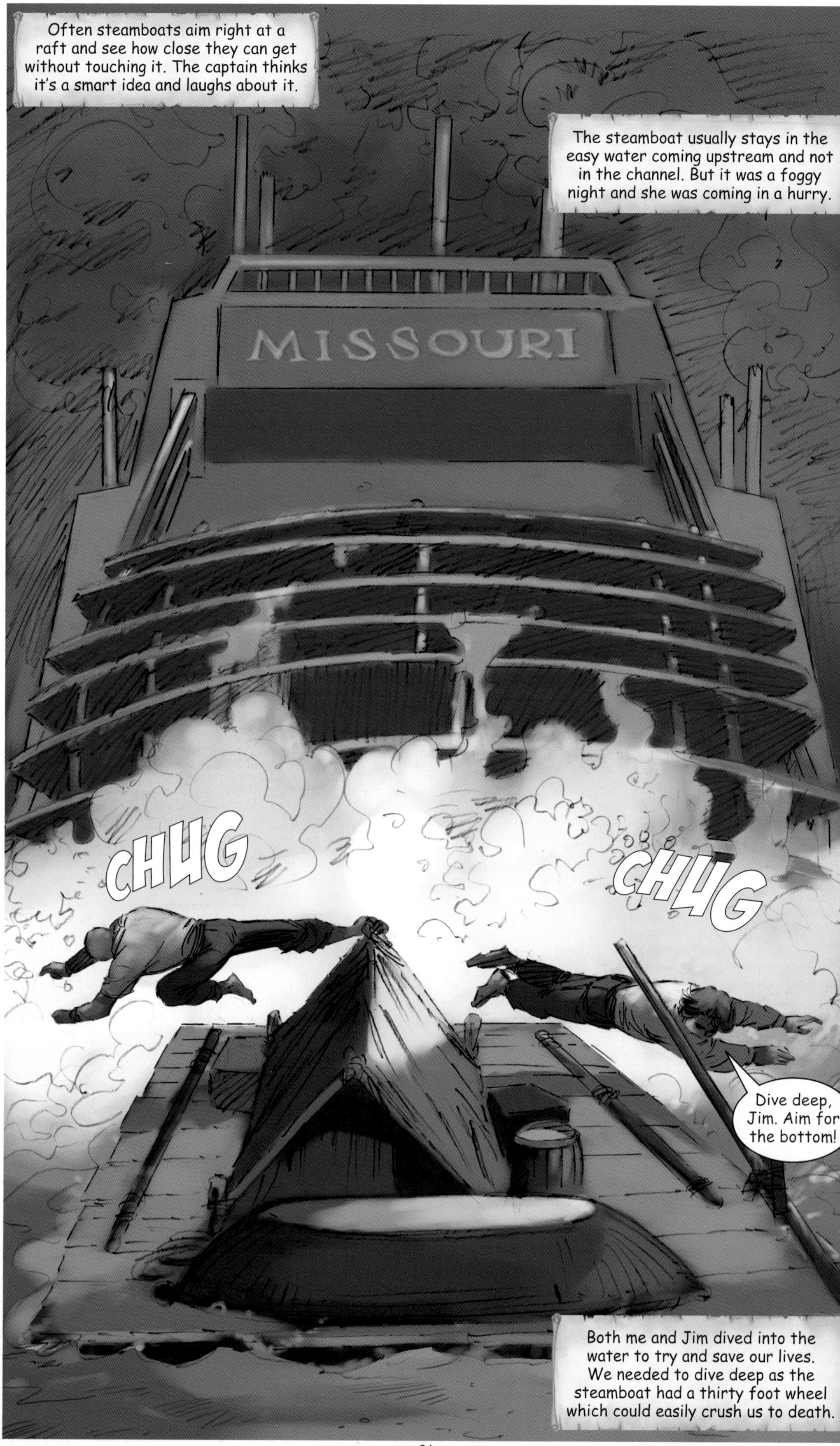

Often steamboats aim right at a raft and see how close they can get without touching it. The captain thinks it's a smart idea and laughs about it.
The steamboat usually stays in the easy water coming upstream and not in the channel. But it was a foggy night and she was coming in a hurry.
MISSOURI
CHUG
CHUG
Dive deep, Jim. Aim for the bottom!
Both me and Jim dived into the water to try and save our lives. We needed to dive deep as the steamboat had a thirty foot wheel which could easily crush us to death.

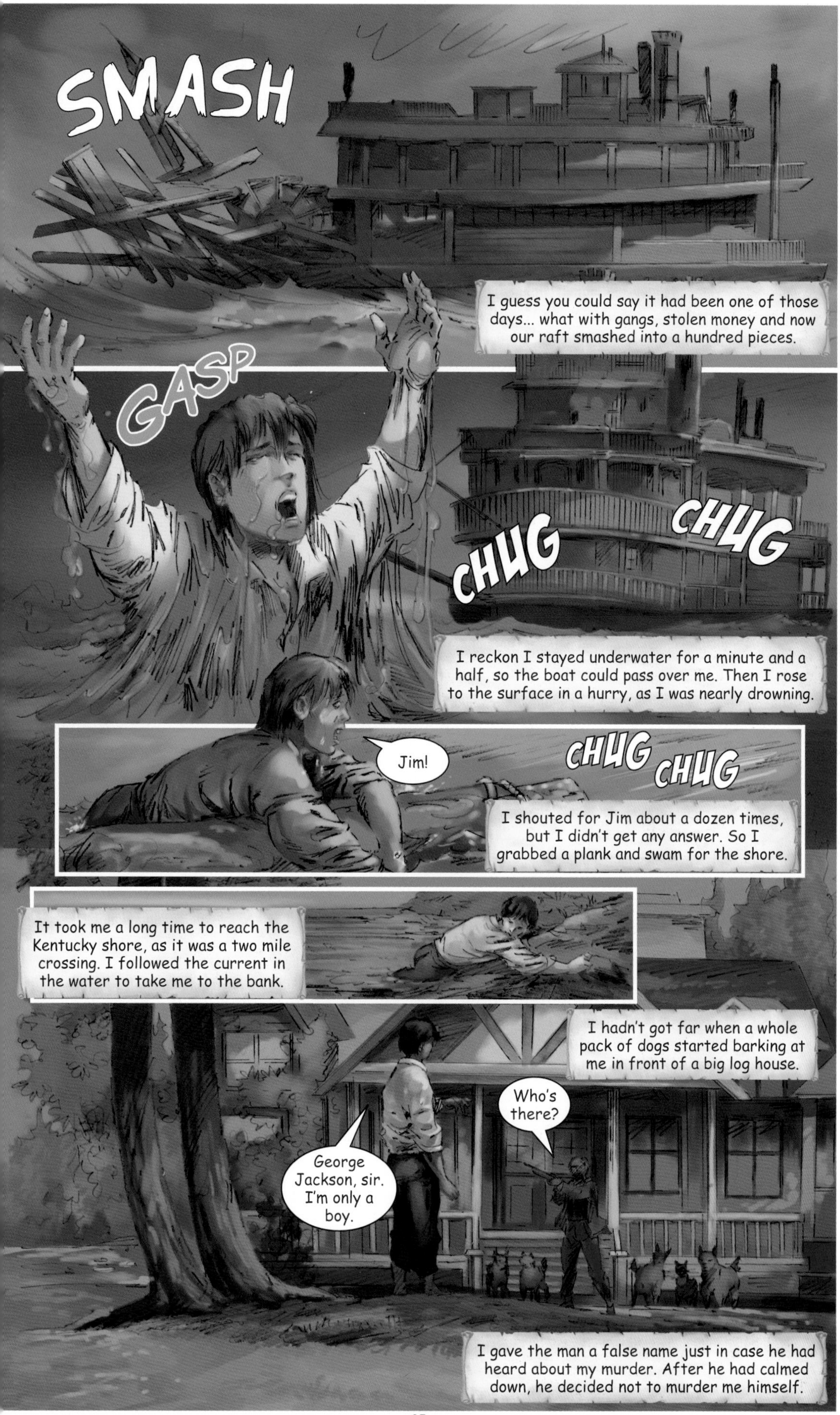
SMASH
I guess you could say it had been one of those days... what with gangs, stolen money and now our raft smashed into a hundred pieces.
GASP
CHUG
CHUG
I reckon I stayed underwater for a minute and a half, so the boat could pass over me. Then I rose to the surface in a hurry, as I was nearly drowning.
Jim!
CHUG
CHUG
I shouted for Jim about a dozen times, but I didn't get any answer. So I grabbed a plank and swam for the shore.
It took me a long time to reach the Kentucky shore, as it was a two mile crossing. I followed the current in the water to take me to the bank.
I hadn't got far when a whole pack of dogs started barking at me in front of a big log house.
Who's there?
George Jackson, sir. I'm only a boy.
I gave the man a false name just in case he had heard about my murder. After he had calmed down, he decided not to murder me himself.

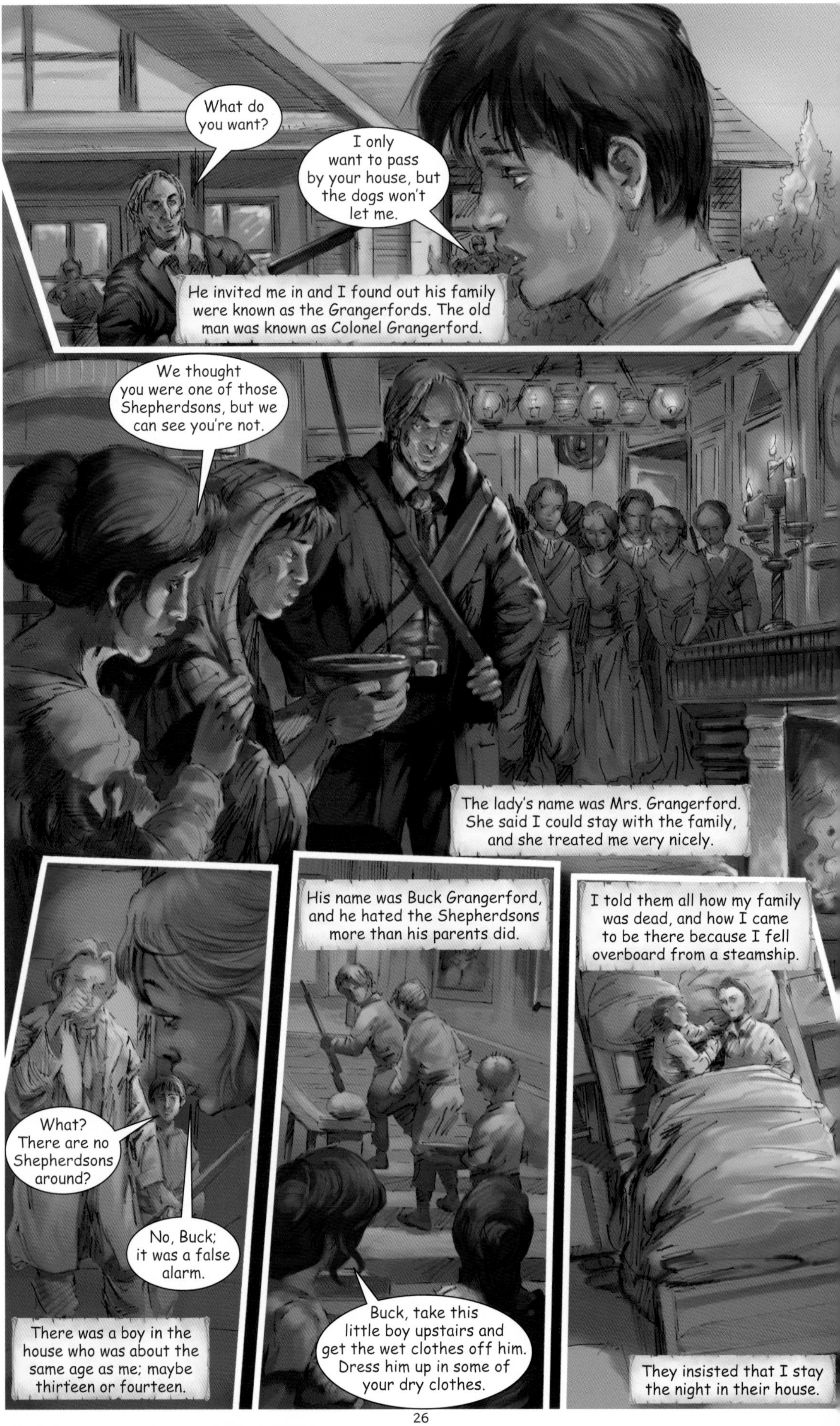

What do you want?
I only want to pass by your house, but the dogs won't let me.
He invited me in and I found out his family were known as the Grangerfords. The old man was known as Colonel Grangerford.
We thought you were one of those Shepherdsons, but we can see you're not.
The lady's name was Mrs. Grangerford. She said I could stay with the family, and she treated me very nicely.
What? There are no Shepherdsons around?
No, Buck; it was a false alarm.
There was a boy in the house who was about the same age as me; maybe thirteen or fourteen.
His name was Buck Grangerford, and he hated the Shepherdsons more than his parents did.
Buck, take this little boy upstairs and get the wet clothes off him. Dress him up in some of your dry clothes.
I told them all how my family was dead, and how I came to be there because I fell overboard from a steamship.
They insisted that I stay the night in their house.

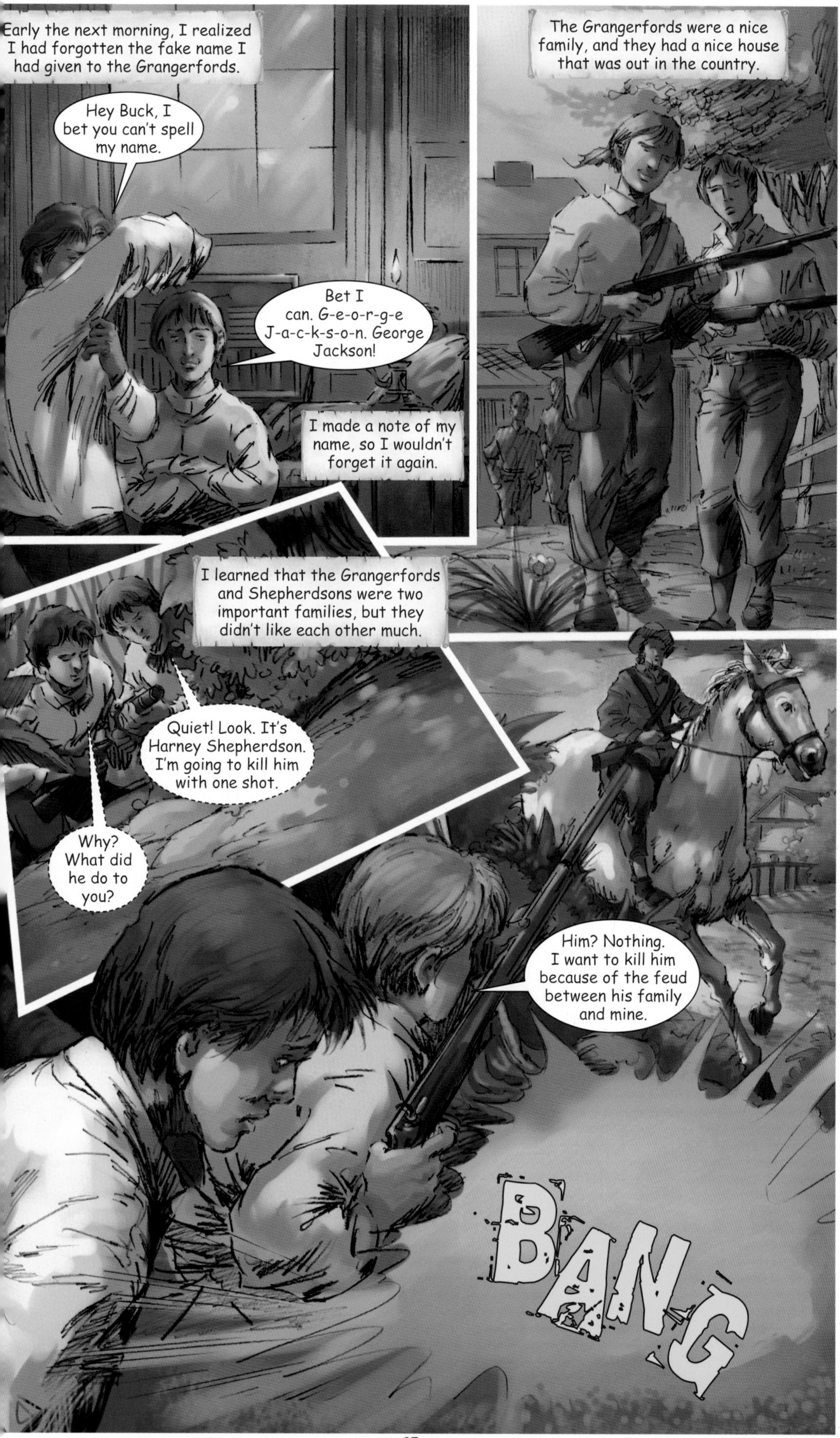
Early the next morning, I realized I had forgotten the fake name I had given to the Grangerfords.
Hey Buck, I bet you can't spell my name.
Bet I can. G-e-o-r-g-e J-a-c-k-s-o-n. George Jackson!
I made a note of my name, so I wouldn't forget it again.
The Grangerfords were a nice family, and they had a nice house that was out in the country.
I learned that the Grangerfords and Shepherdsons were two important families, but they didn't like each other much.
Quiet! Look. It's Harney Shepherdson. I'm going to kill him with one shot.
Why? What did he do to you?
Him? Nothing. I want to kill him because of the feud between his family and mine.
BANG

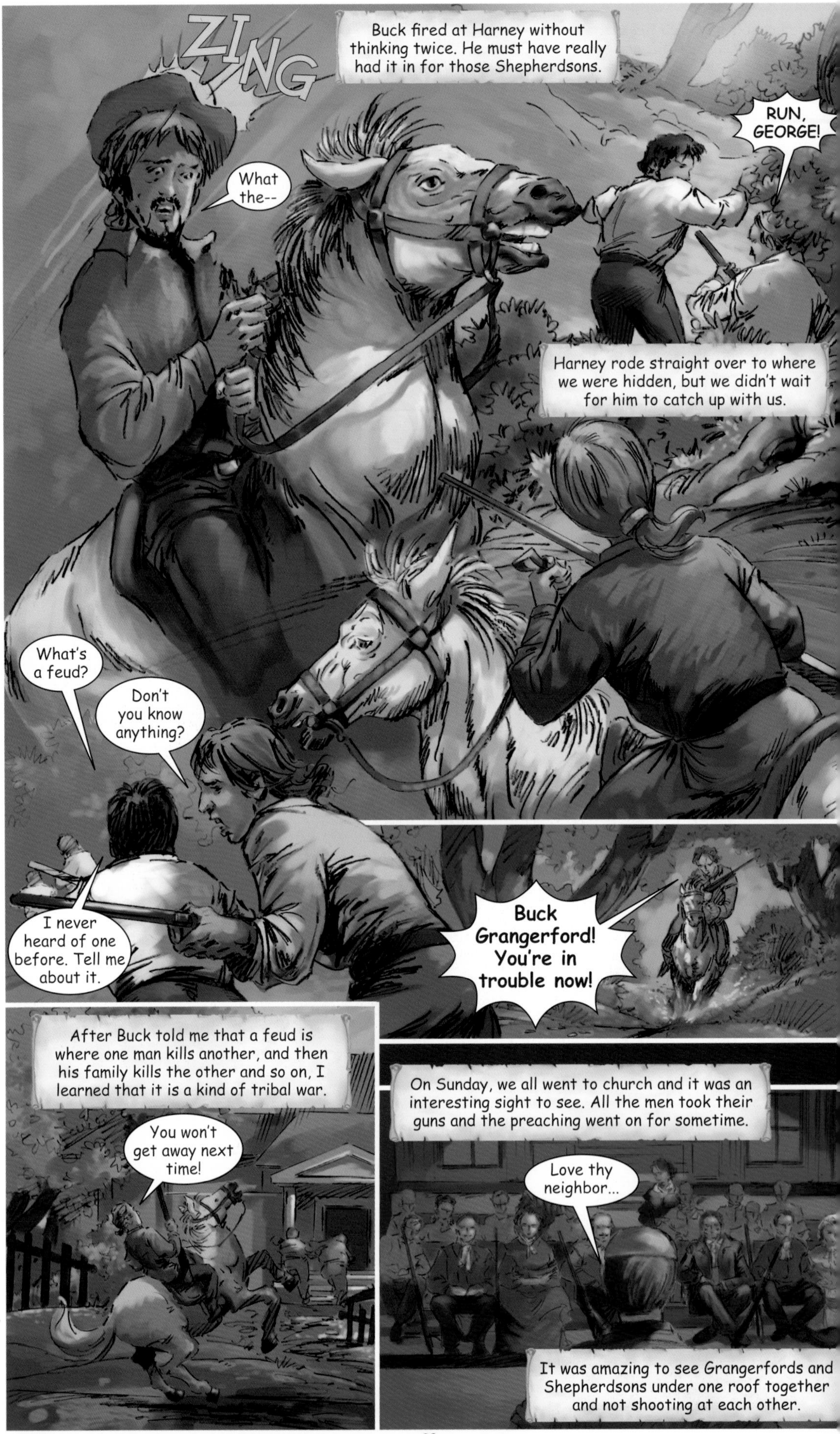
ZING
Buck fired at Harney without thinking twice. He must have really had it in for those Shepherdsons.
What the--
RUN, GEORGE!
Harney rode straight over to where we were hidden, but we didn't wait for him to catch up with us.
What's a feud?
Don't you know anything?
I never heard of one before. Tell me about it.
Buck Grangerford! You're in trouble now!
After Buck told me that a feud is where one man kills another, and then his family kills the other and so on, I learned that it is a kind of tribal war.
You won't get away next time!
On Sunday, we all went to church and it was an interesting sight to see. All the men took their guns and the preaching went on for sometime.
Love thy neighbor...
It was amazing to see Grangerfords and Shepherdsons under one roof together and not shooting at each other.

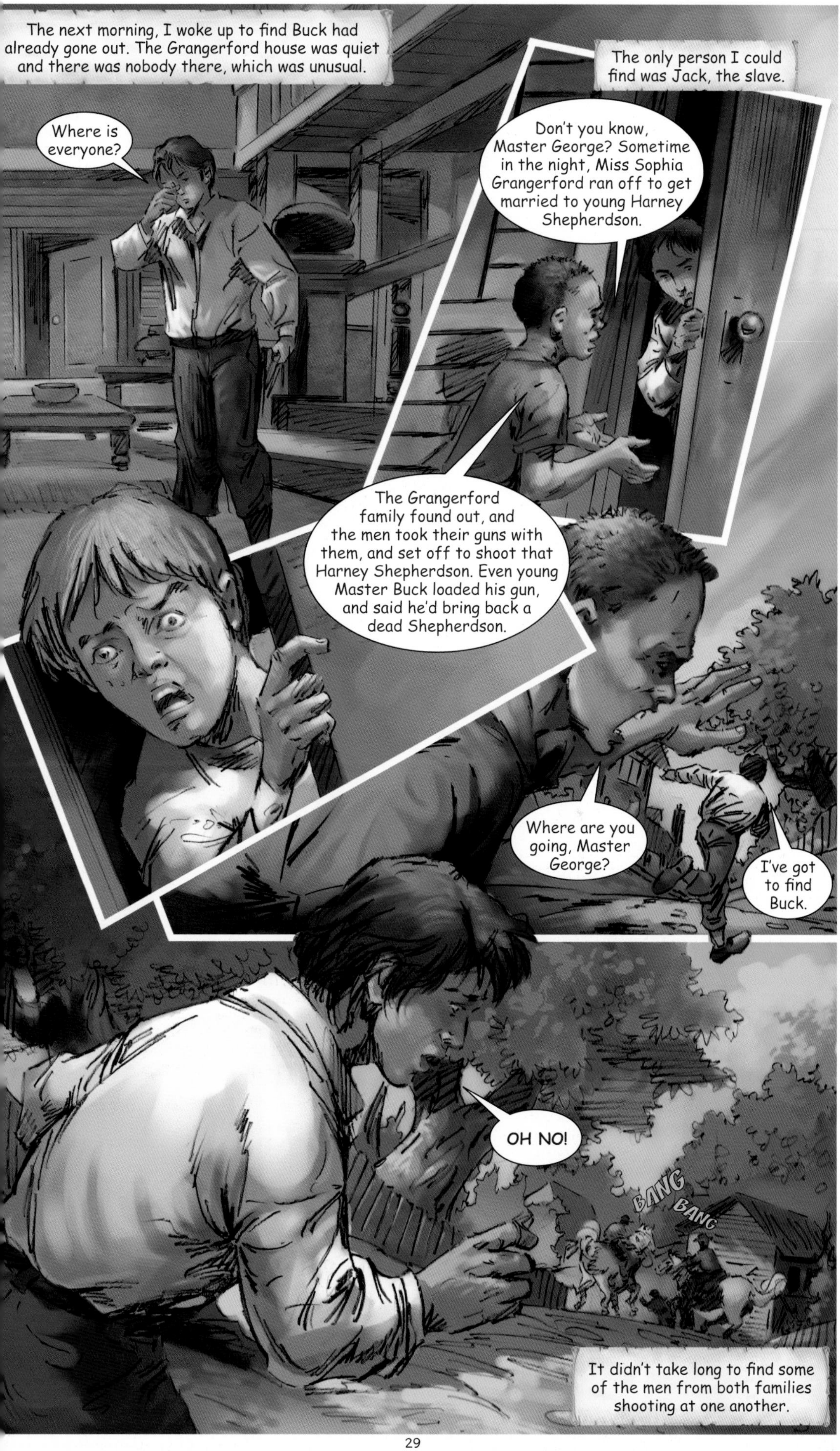
The next morning, I woke up to find Buck had already gone out. The Grangerford house was quiet and there was nobody there, which was unusual.
Where is everyone?
The only person I could find was Jack, the slave.
Don't you know, Master George? Sometime in the night, Miss Sophia Grangerford ran off to get married to young Harney Shepherdson.
The Grangerford family found out, and the men took their guns with them, and set off to shoot that Harney Shepherdson. Even young Master Buck loaded his gun, and said he'd bring back a dead Shepherdson.
Where are you going, Master George?
I've got to find Buck.
OH NO!
BANG
BANG
It didn't take long to find some of the men from both families shooting at one another.

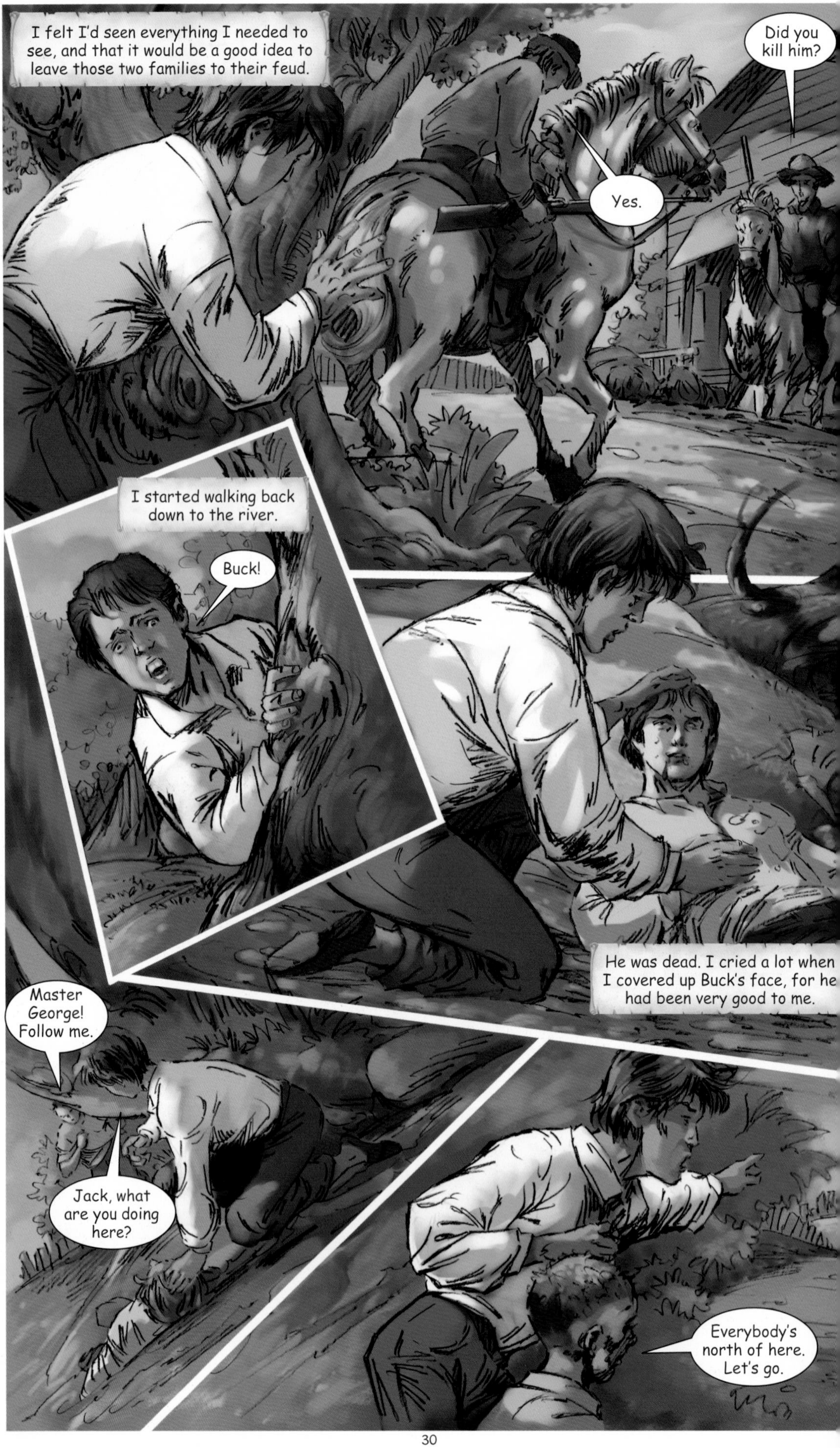

I felt I'd seen everything I needed to see, and that it would be a good idea to leave those two families to their feud.
Did you kill him?
Yes.
I started walking back down to the river.
Buck!
He was dead. I cried a lot when I covered up Buck's face, for he had been very good to me.
Master George! Follow me.
Jack, what are you doing here?
Everybody's north of here. Let's go.

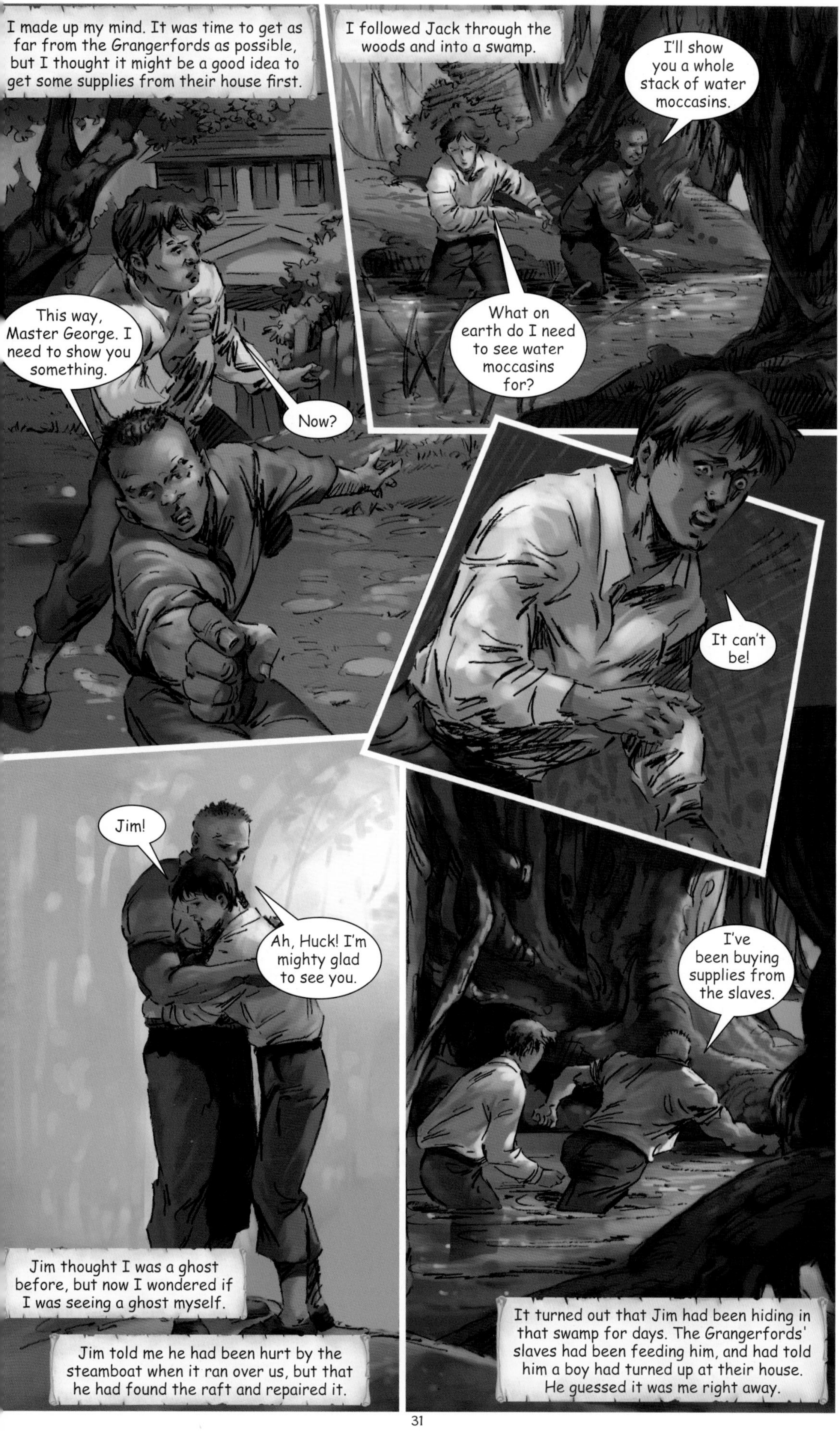
I made up my mind. It was time to get as far from the Grangerfords as possible, but I thought it might be a good idea to get some supplies from their house first.
This way, Master George. I need to show you something.
Now?
I followed Jack through the woods and into a swamp.
I'll show you a whole stack of water moccasins.
What on earth do I need to see water moccasins for?
It can't be!
Jim!
Ah, Huck! I'm mighty glad to see you.
Jim thought I was a ghost before, but now I wondered if I was seeing a ghost myself.
Jim told me he had been hurt by the steamboat when it ran over us, but that he had found the raft and repaired it.
I've been buying supplies from the slaves.
It turned out that Jim had been hiding in that swamp for days. The Grangerfords' slaves had been feeding him, and had told him a boy had turned up at their house. He guessed it was me right away.

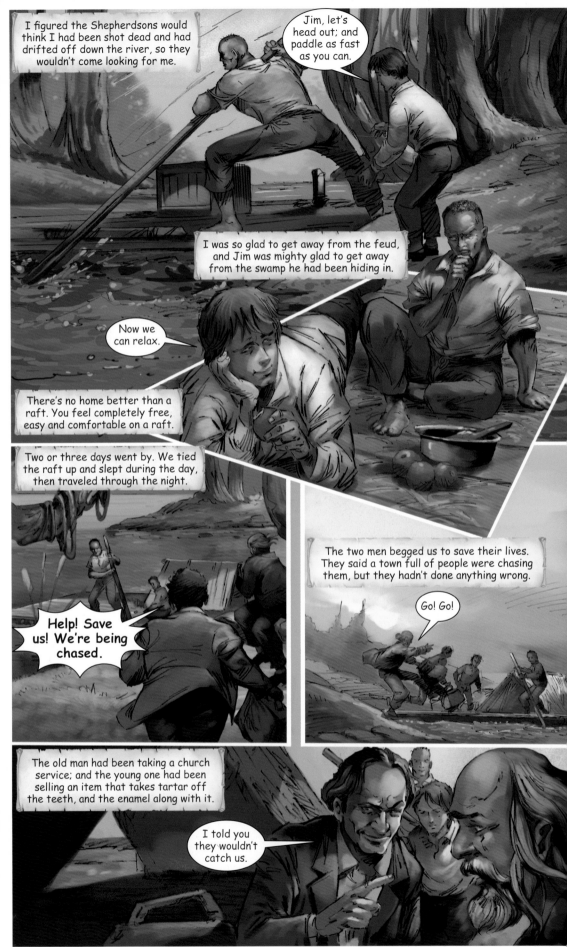

I figured the Shepherdsons would think I had been shot dead and had drifted off down the river, so they wouldn't come looking for me.

Jim, let's head out; and paddle as fast as you can.

I was so glad to get away from the feud, and Jim was mighty glad to get away from the swamp he had been hiding in.

Now we can relax.

There's no home better than a raft. You feel completely free, easy and comfortable on a raft.

Two or three days went by. We tied the raft up and slept during the day, then traveled through the night.

Help! Save us! We're being chased.

The two men begged us to save their lives. They said a town full of people were chasing them, but they hadn't done anything wrong.

Go! Go!

The old man had been taking a church service; and the young one had been selling an item that takes tartar off the teeth, and the enamel along with it.

I told you they wouldn't catch us.

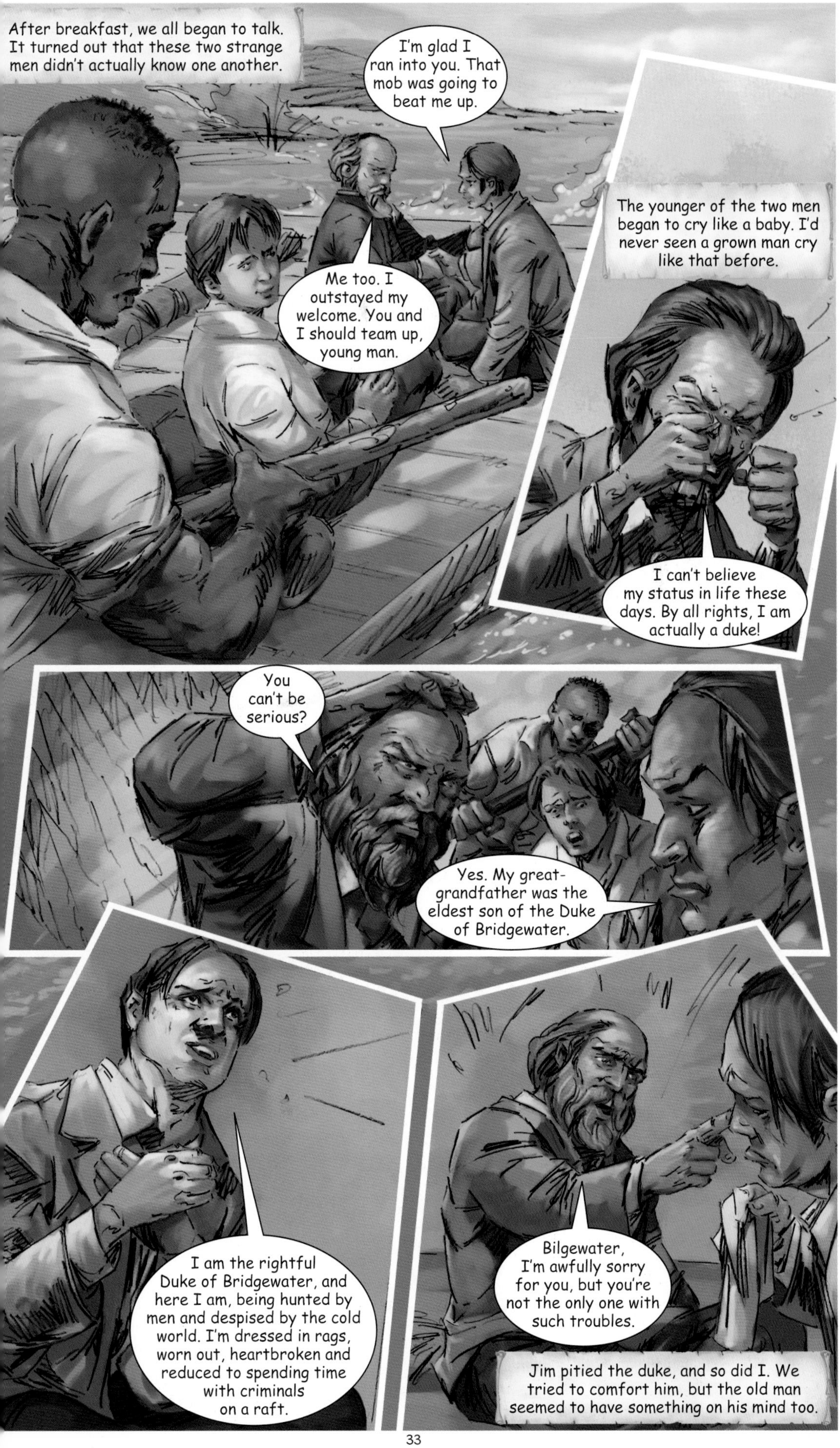
After breakfast, we all began to talk. It turned out that these two strange men didn't actually know one another.
I'm glad I ran into you. That mob was going to beat me up.
Me too. I outstayed my welcome. You and I should team up, young man.
The younger of the two men began to cry like a baby. I'd never seen a grown man cry like that before.
I can't believe my status in life these days. By all rights, I am actually a duke!
You can't be serious?
Yes. My great-grandfather was the eldest son of the Duke of Bridgewater.
I am the rightful Duke of Bridgewater, and here I am, being hunted by men and despised by the cold world. I'm dressed in rags, worn out, heartbroken and reduced to spending time with criminals on a raft.
Bilgewater, I'm awfully sorry for you, but you're not the only one with such troubles.
Jim pitied the duke, and so did I. We tried to comfort him, but the old man seemed to have something on his mind too.

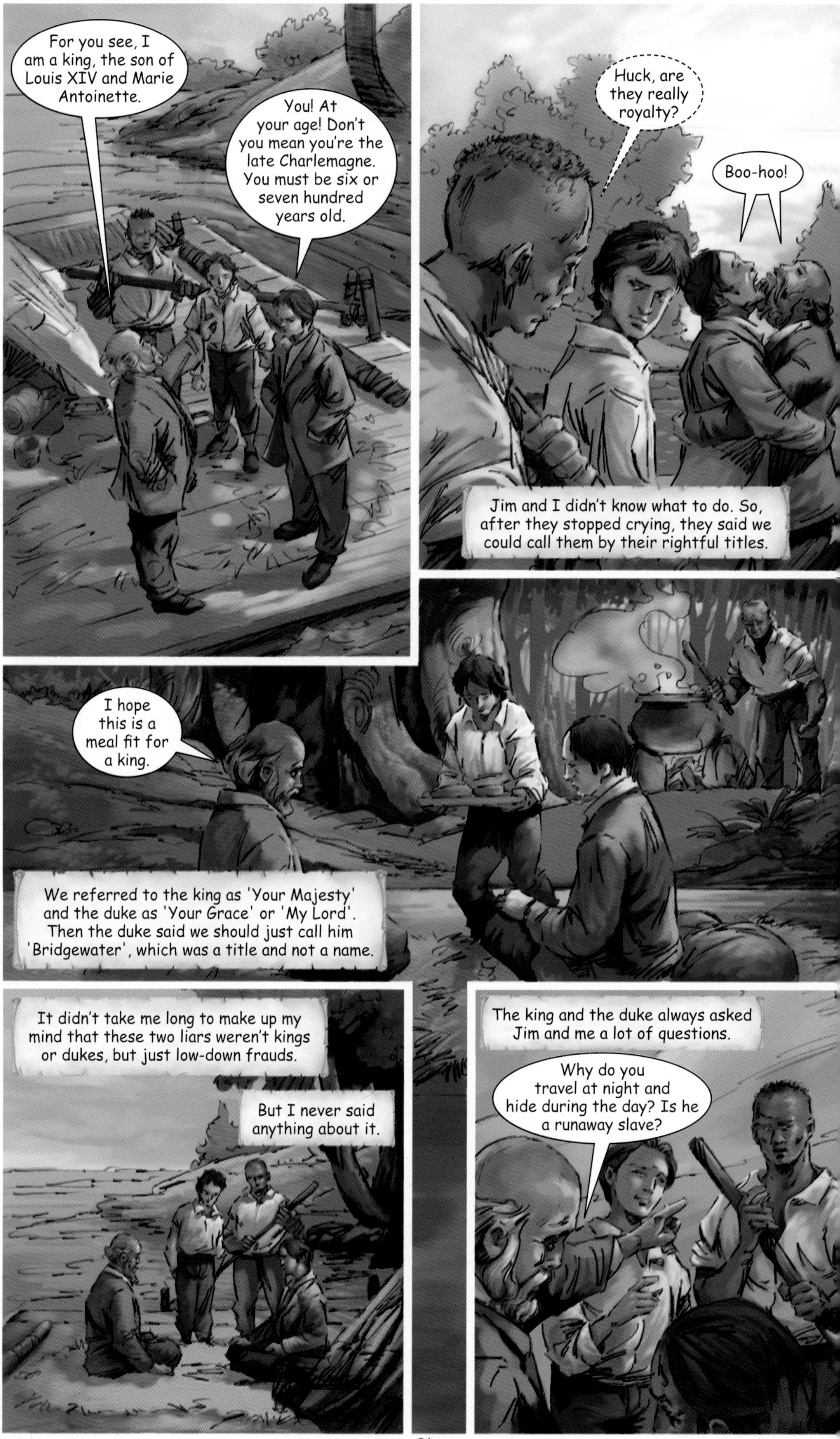
For you see, I am a king, the son of Louis XIV and Marie Antoinette.
You! At your age! Don't you mean you're the late Charlemagne. You must be six or seven hundred years old.
Huck, are they really royalty?
Boo-hoo!
Jim and I didn't know what to do. So, after they stopped crying, they said we could call them by their rightful titles.
I hope this is a meal fit for a king.
We referred to the king as 'Your Majesty' and the duke as 'Your Grace' or 'My Lord'. Then the duke said we should just call him 'Bridgewater', which was a title and not a name.
It didn't take me long to make up my mind that these two liars weren't kings or dukes, but just low-down frauds.
But I never said anything about it.
The king and the duke always asked Jim and me a lot of questions.
Why do you travel at night and hide during the day? Is he a runaway slave?

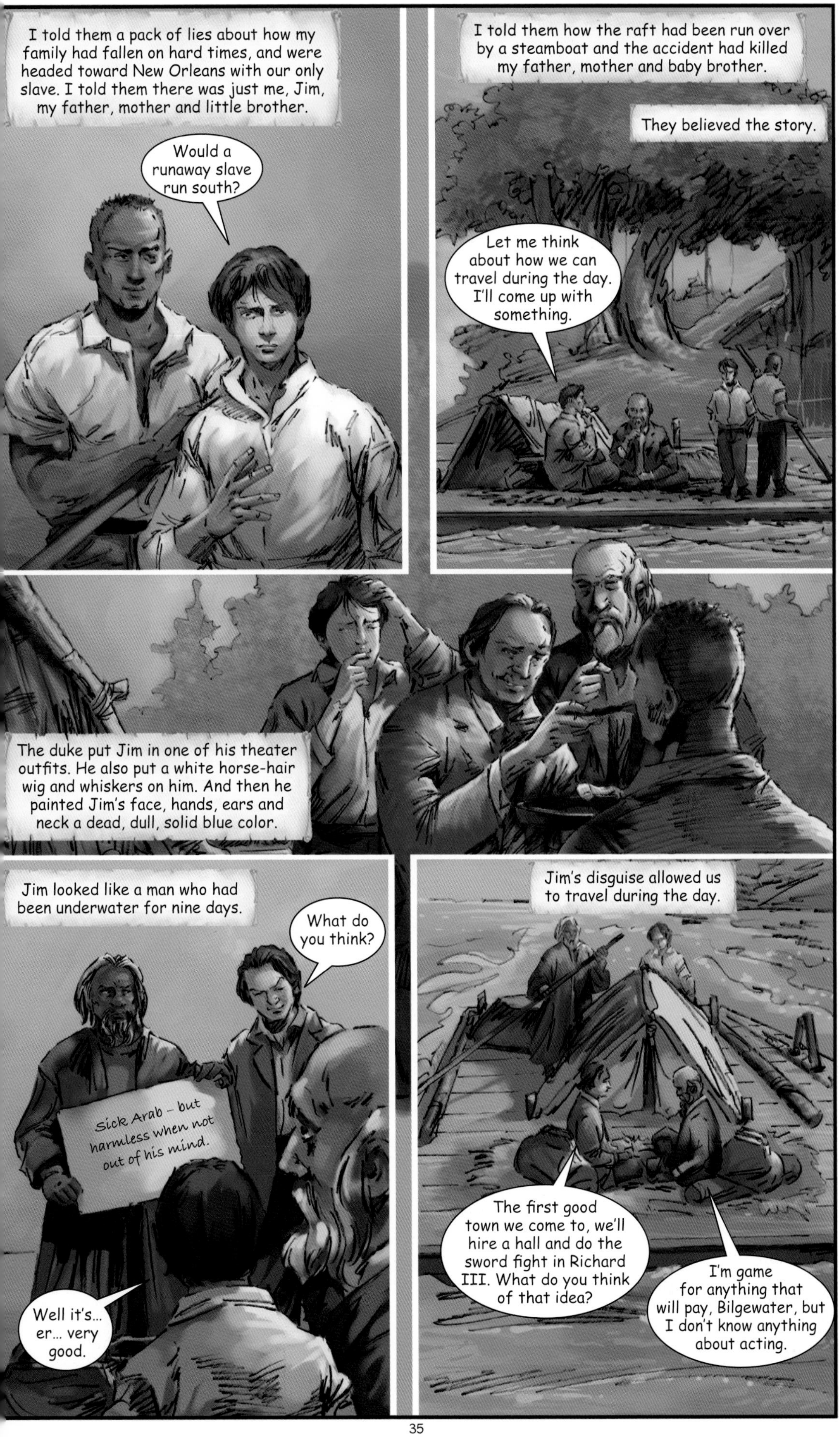
I told them a pack of lies about how my family had fallen on hard times, and were headed toward New Orleans with our only slave. I told them there was just me, Jim, my father, mother and little brother.
Would a runaway slave run south?
I told them how the raft had been run over by a steamboat and the accident had killed my father, mother and baby brother.
They believed the story.
Let me think about how we can travel during the day. I'll come up with something.
The duke put Jim in one of his theater outfits. He also put a white horse-hair wig and whiskers on him. And then he painted Jim's face, hands, ears and neck a dead, dull, solid blue color.
Jim looked like a man who had been underwater for nine days.
What do you think?
Sick Arab – but harmless when not out of his mind.
Well it's... er... very good.
Jim's disguise allowed us to travel during the day.
The first good town we come to, we'll hire a hall and do the sword fight in Richard III. What do you think of that idea?
I'm game for anything that will pay, Bilgewater, but I don't know anything about acting.

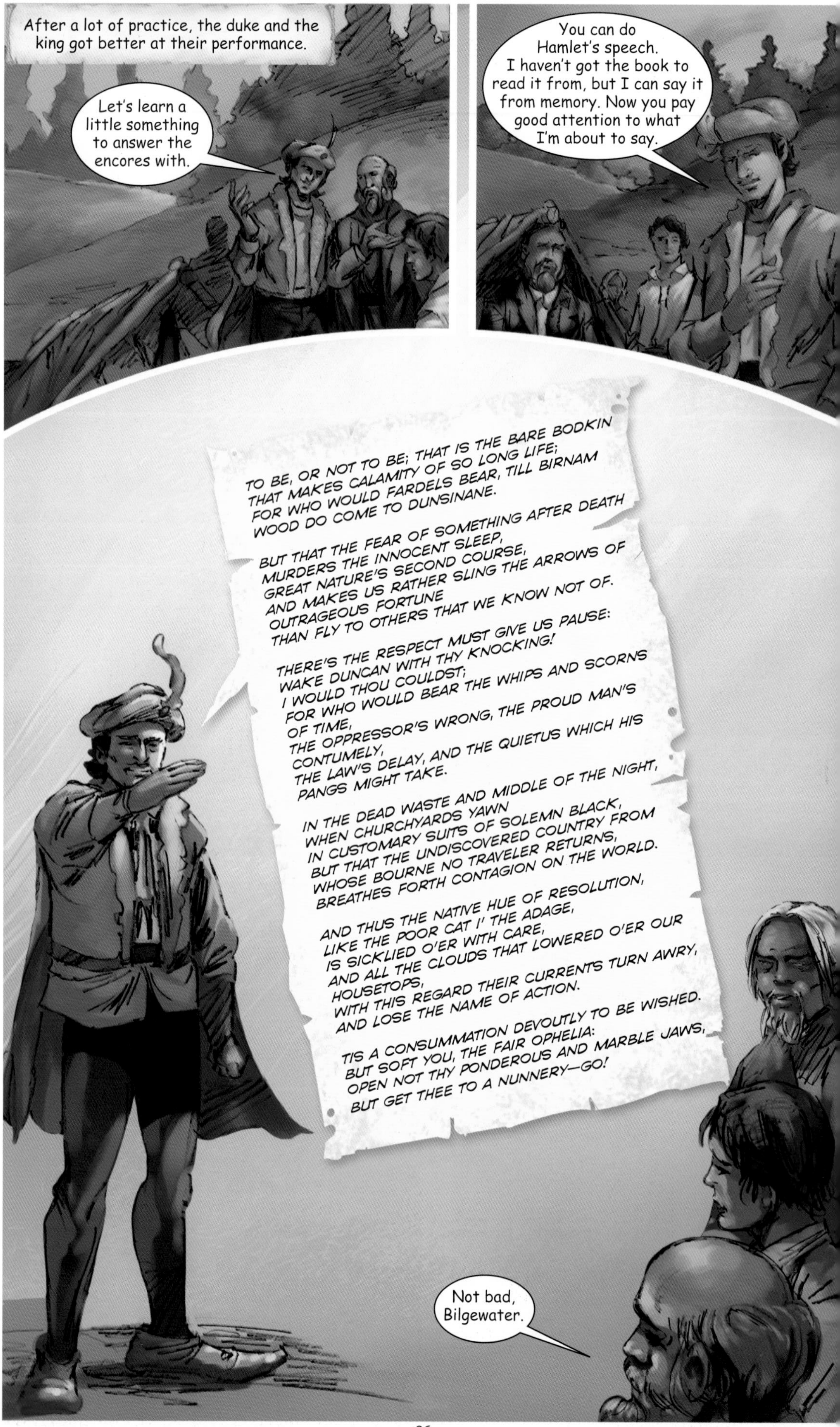
After a lot of practice, the duke and the king got better at their performance.
Let's learn a little something to answer the encores with.
You can do Hamlet's speech. I haven't got the book to read it from, but I can say it from memory. Now you pay good attention to what I'm about to say.
TO BE, OR NOT TO BE; THAT IS THE BARE BODKIN
THAT MAKES CALAMITY OF SO LONG LIFE;
FOR WHO WOULD FARDELS BEAR, TILL BIRNAM
WOOD DO COME TO DUNSINANE.
BUT THAT THE FEAR OF SOMETHING AFTER DEATH
MURDERS THE INNOCENT SLEEP,
GREAT NATURE'S SECOND COURSE,
AND MAKES US RATHER SLING THE ARROWS OF
OUTRAGEOUS FORTUNE
THAN FLY TO OTHERS THAT WE KNOW NOT OF.
THERE'S THE RESPECT MUST GIVE US PAUSE:
WAKE DUNCAN WITH THY KNOCKING!
I WOULD THOU COULDST;
FOR WHO WOULD BEAR THE WHIPS AND SCORNS
OF TIME,
THE OPPRESSOR'S WRONG, THE PROUD MAN'S
CONTUMELY,
THE LAW'S DELAY, AND THE QUIETUS WHICH HIS
PANGS MIGHT TAKE.
IN THE DEAD WASTE AND MIDDLE OF THE NIGHT,
WHEN CHURCHYARDS YAWN
IN CUSTOMARY SUITS OF SOLEMN BLACK,
BUT THAT THE UNDISCOVERED COUNTRY FROM
WHOSE BOURNE NO TRAVELER RETURNS,
BREATHES FORTH CONTAGION ON THE WORLD.
AND THUS THE NATIVE HUE OF RESOLUTION,
LIKE THE POOR CAT I' THE ADAGE,
IS SICKLIED O'ER WITH CARE,
AND ALL THE CLOUDS THAT LOWERED O'ER OUR
HOUSETOPS,
WITH THIS REGARD THEIR CURRENTS TURN AWRY,
AND LOSE THE NAME OF ACTION.
TIS A CONSUMMATION DEVOUTLY TO BE WISHED.
BUT SOFT YOU, THE FAIR OPHELIA:
OPEN NOT THY PONDEROUS AND MARBLE JAWS,
BUT GET THEE TO A NUNNERY—GO!
Not bad, Bilgewater.

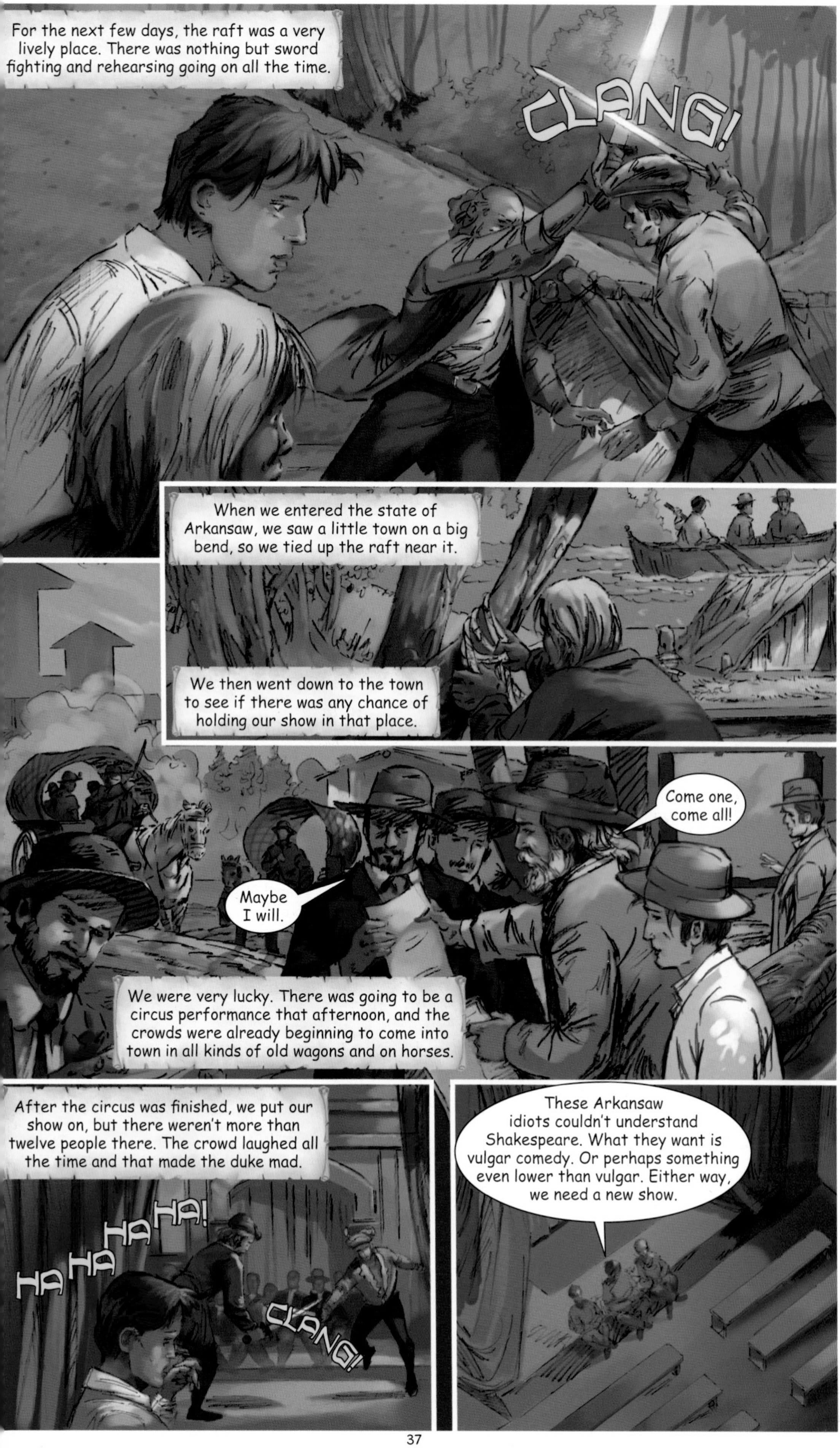
For the next few days, the raft was a very lively place. There was nothing but sword fighting and rehearsing going on all the time.
CLANG!
When we entered the state of Arkansaw, we saw a little town on a big bend, so we tied up the raft near it.
We then went down to the town to see if there was any chance of holding our show in that place.
Come one, come all!
Maybe I will.
We were very lucky. There was going to be a circus performance that afternoon, and the crowds were already beginning to come into town in all kinds of old wagons and on horses.
After the circus was finished, we put our show on, but there weren't more than twelve people there. The crowd laughed all the time and that made the duke mad.
HA HA HA HA!
CLANG!
These Arkansaw idiots couldn't understand Shakespeare. What they want is vulgar comedy. Or perhaps something even lower than vulgar. Either way, we need a new show.

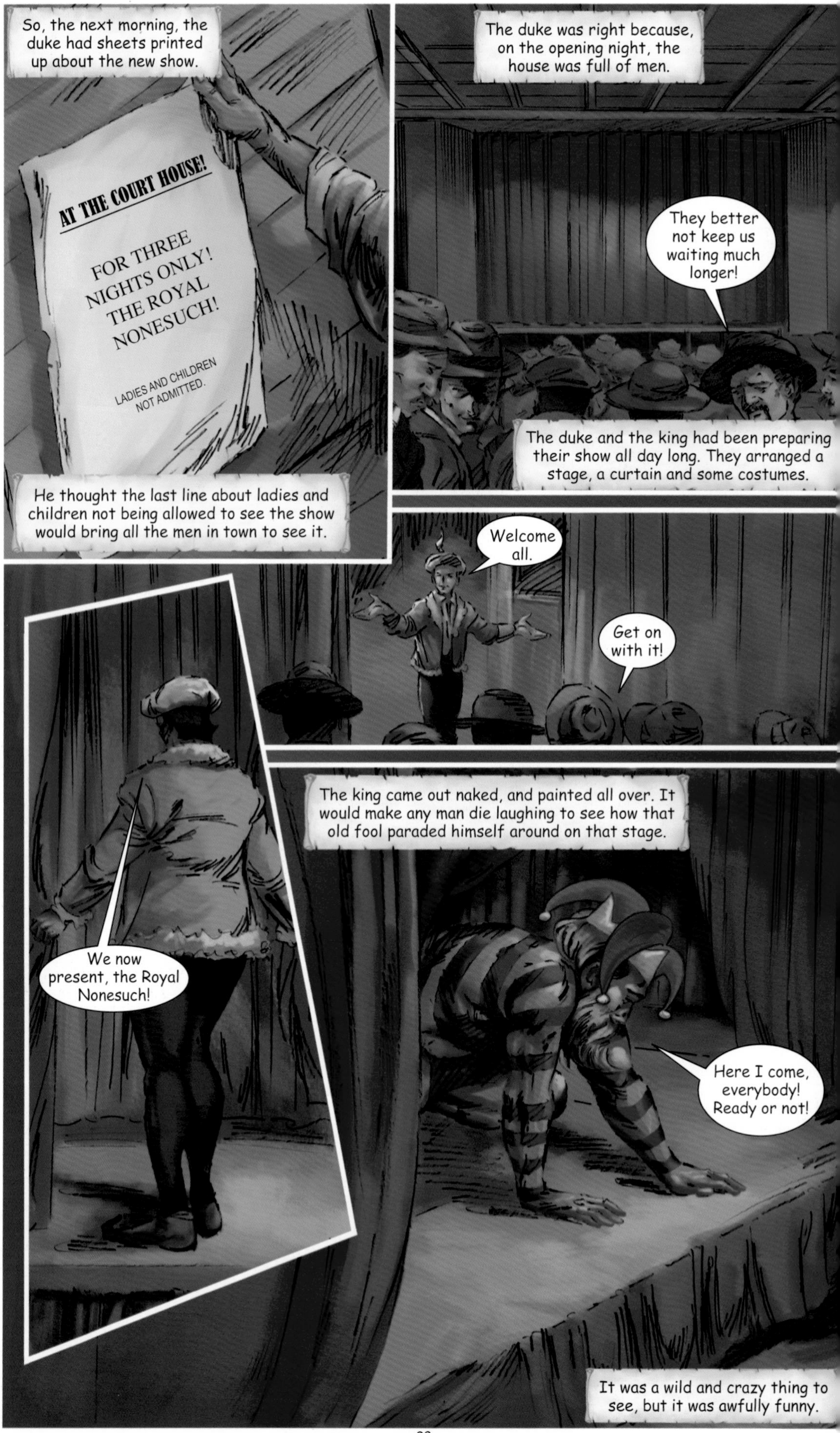
So, the next morning, the duke had sheets printed up about the new show.
AT THE COURT HOUSE!
FOR THREE NIGHTS ONLY! THE ROYAL NONESUCH!
LADIES AND CHILDREN NOT ADMITTED.
He thought the last line about ladies and children not being allowed to see the show would bring all the men in town to see it.
The duke was right because, on the opening night, the house was full of men.
They better not keep us waiting much longer!
The duke and the king had been preparing their show all day long. They arranged a stage, a curtain and some costumes.
Welcome all.
Get on with it!
We now present, the Royal Nonesuch!
The king came out naked, and painted all over. It would make any man die laughing to see how that old fool paraded himself around on that stage.
Here I come, everybody! Ready or not!
It was a wild and crazy thing to see, but it was awfully funny.

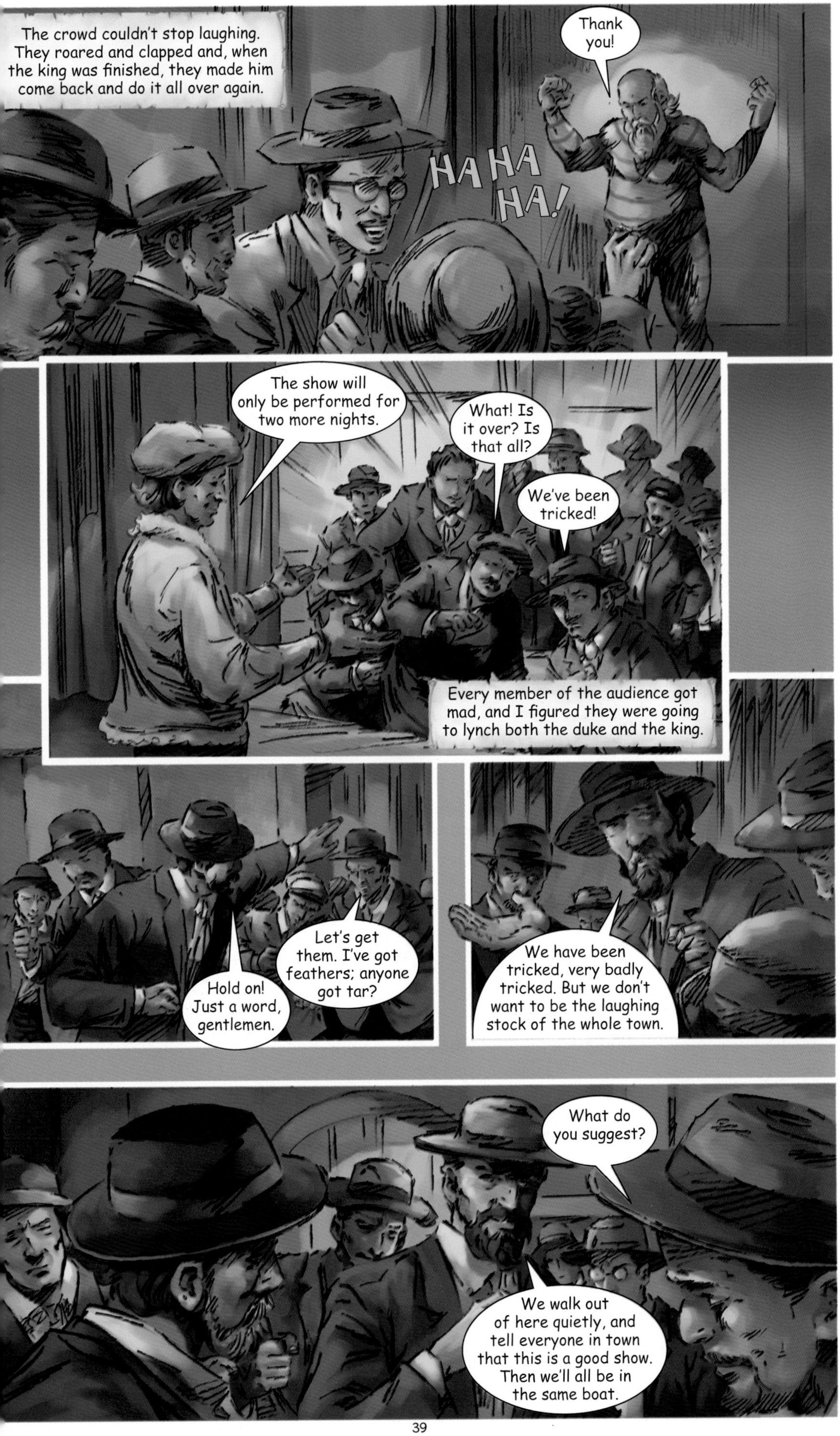
The crowd couldn't stop laughing. They roared and clapped and, when the king was finished, they made him come back and do it all over again.
Thank you!
HA HA HA!
The show will only be performed for two more nights.
What! Is it over? Is that all?
We've been tricked!
Every member of the audience got mad, and I figured they were going to lynch both the duke and the king.
Hold on! Just a word, gentlemen.
Let's get them. I've got feathers; anyone got tar?
We have been tricked, very badly tricked. But we don't want to be the laughing stock of the whole town.
What do you suggest?
We walk out of here quietly, and tell everyone in town that this is a good show. Then we'll all be in the same boat.

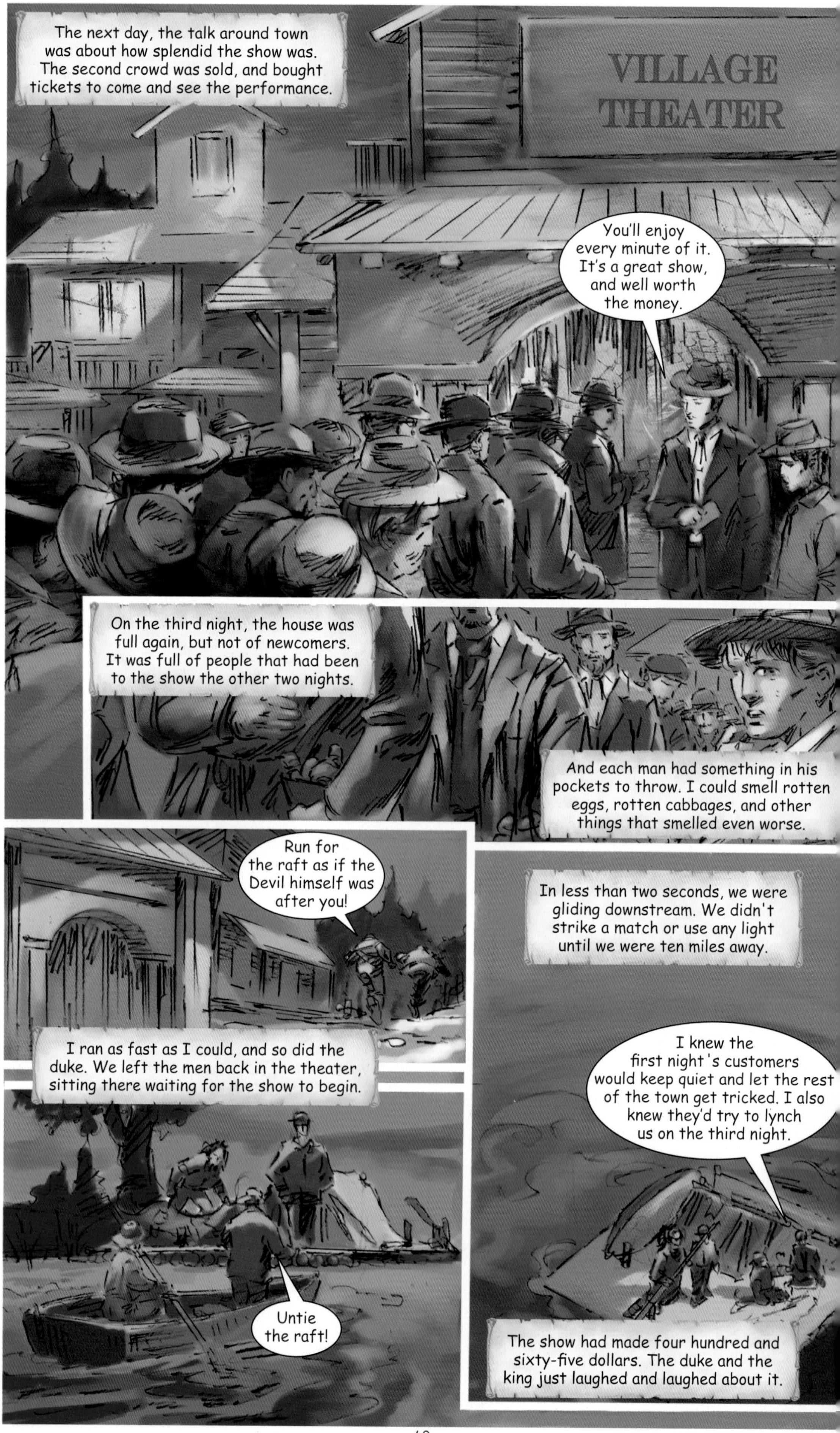

The next day, the talk around town was about how splendid the show was. The second crowd was sold, and bought tickets to come and see the performance.
VILLAGE THEATER
You'll enjoy every minute of it. It's a great show, and well worth the money.
On the third night, the house was full again, but not of newcomers. It was full of people that had been to the show the other two nights.
And each man had something in his pockets to throw. I could smell rotten eggs, rotten cabbages, and other things that smelled even worse.
Run for the raft as if the Devil himself was after you!
I ran as fast as I could, and so did the duke. We left the men back in the theater, sitting there waiting for the show to begin.
Untie the raft!
In less than two seconds, we were gliding downstream. We didn't strike a match or use any light until we were ten miles away.
I knew the first night's customers would keep quiet and let the rest of the town get tricked. I also knew they'd try to lynch us on the third night.
The show had made four hundred and sixty-five dollars. The duke and the king just laughed and laughed about it.

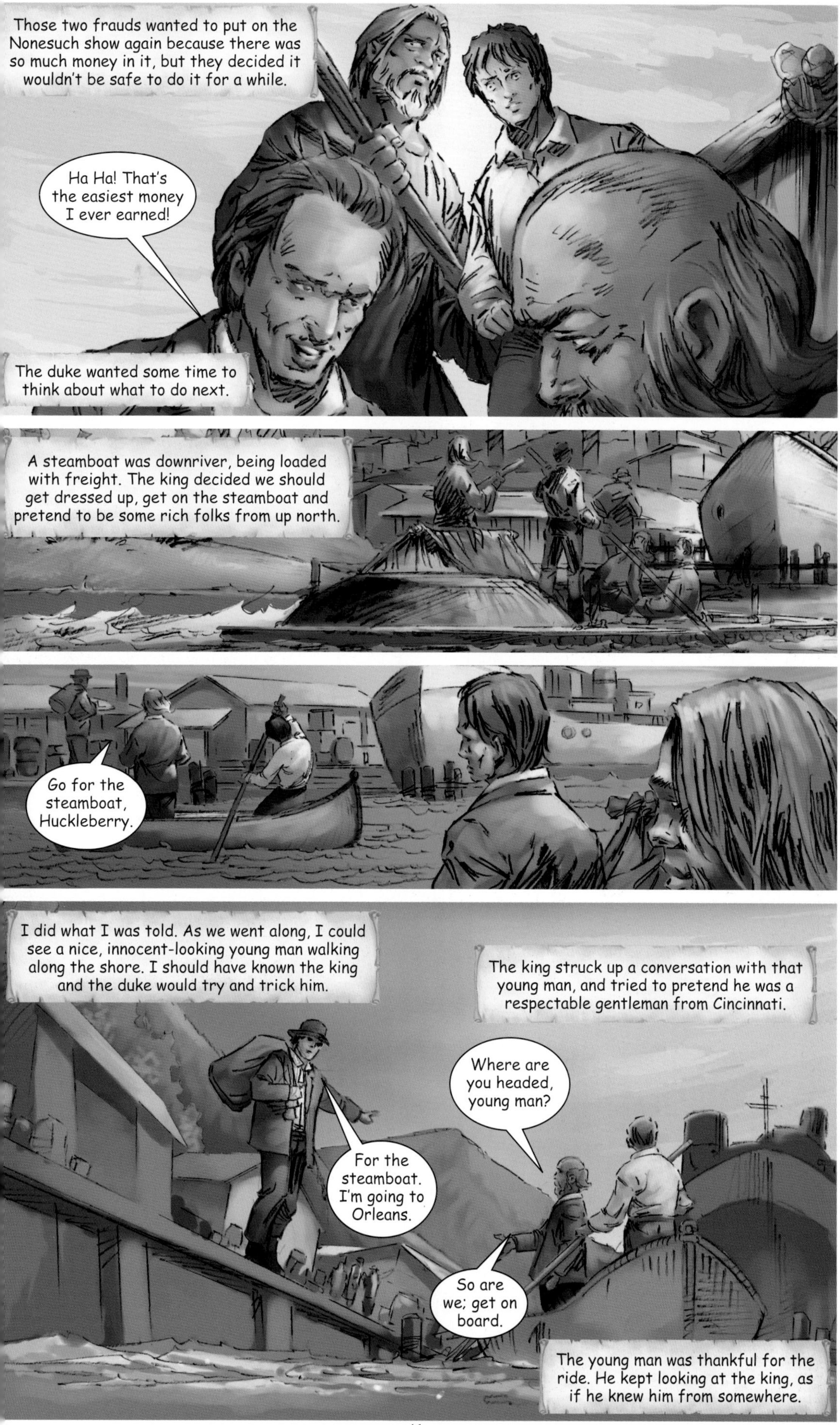
Those two frauds wanted to put on the Nonesuch show again because there was so much money in it, but they decided it wouldn't be safe to do it for a while.
Ha Ha! That's the easiest money I ever earned!
The duke wanted some time to think about what to do next.
A steamboat was downriver, being loaded with freight. The king decided we should get dressed up, get on the steamboat and pretend to be some rich folks from up north.
Go for the steamboat, Huckleberry.
I did what I was told. As we went along, I could see a nice, innocent-looking young man walking along the shore. I should have known the king and the duke would try and trick him.
The king struck up a conversation with that young man, and tried to pretend he was a respectable gentleman from Cincinnati.
Where are you headed, young man?
For the steamboat. I'm going to Orleans.
So are we; get on board.
The young man was thankful for the ride. He kept looking at the king, as if he knew him from somewhere.

You know, when I first saw you, I said to myself, 'It's Mr. Harvey Wilks. I'm sure of it.' But then I said, 'No, it can't be him, because he wouldn't be paddling in the river.'

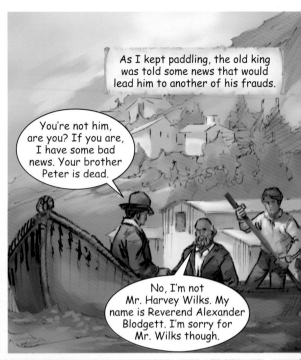

As I kept paddling, the old king was told some news that would lead him to another of his frauds.

You're not him, are you? If you are, I have some bad news. Your brother Peter is dead.

No, I'm not Mr. Harvey Wilks. My name is Reverend Alexander Blodgett. I'm sorry for Mr. Wilks though.

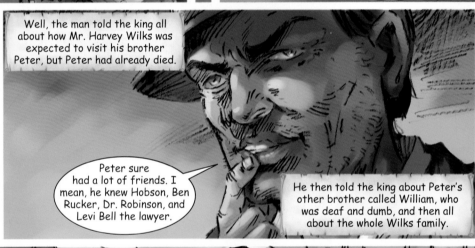

Well, the man told the king all about how Mr. Harvey Wilks was expected to visit his brother Peter, but Peter had already died.

Peter sure had a lot of friends. I mean, he knew Hobson, Ben Rucker, Dr. Robinson, and Levi Bell the lawyer.

He then told the king about Peter's other brother called William, who was deaf and dumb, and then all about the whole Wilks family.

The king listened and kept on asking questions until he knew everything. He was particularly interested when he heard that Peter Wilks had a lot of money and property.

Alright, let's get going. Hurry up.

When he got back to the raft, the king told the duke he had a plan to make a lot of money, and that we should get on a steamboat that was headed downstream.

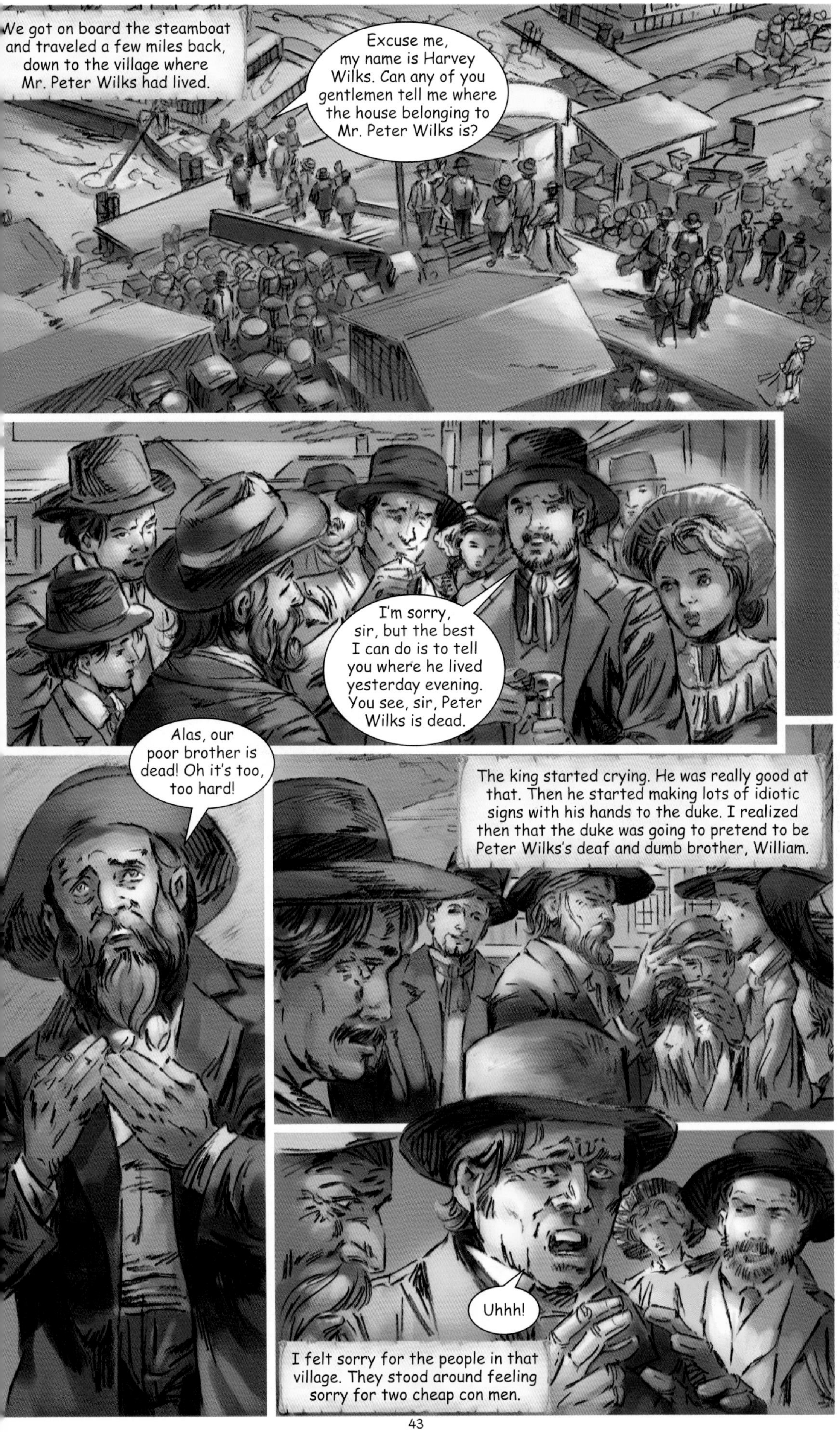
We got on board the steamboat and traveled a few miles back, down to the village where Mr. Peter Wilks had lived.
Excuse me, my name is Harvey Wilks. Can any of you gentlemen tell me where the house belonging to Mr. Peter Wilks is?
I'm sorry, sir, but the best I can do is to tell you where he lived yesterday evening. You see, sir, Peter Wilks is dead.
Alas, our poor brother is dead! Oh it's too, too hard!
The king started crying. He was really good at that. Then he started making lots of idiotic signs with his hands to the duke. I realized then that the duke was going to pretend to be Peter Wilks's deaf and dumb brother, William.
Uhhh!
I felt sorry for the people in that village. They stood around feeling sorry for two cheap con men.

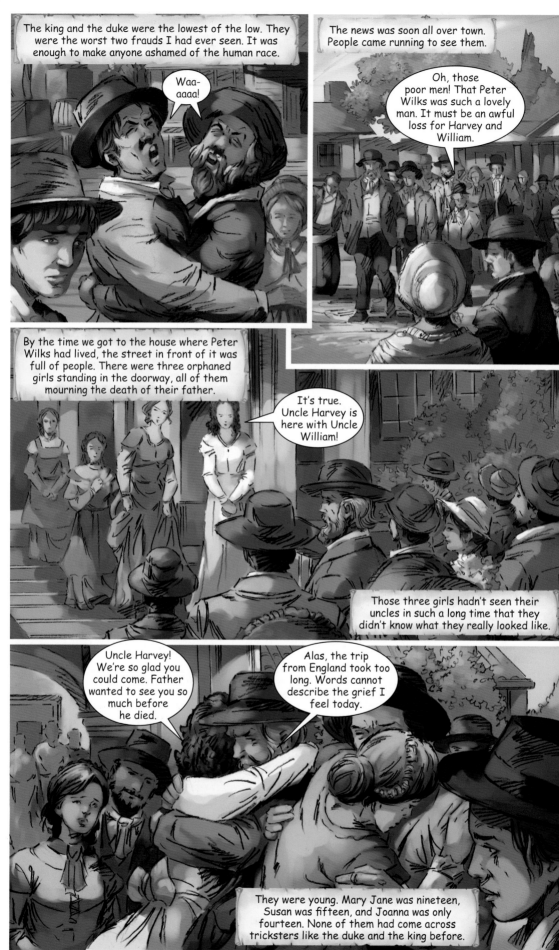

The king and the duke were the lowest of the low. They were the worst two frauds I had ever seen. It was enough to make anyone ashamed of the human race.

Waa-aaaa!

The news was soon all over town. People came running to see them.

Oh, those poor men! That Peter Wilks was such a lovely man. It must be an awful loss for Harvey and William.

By the time we got to the house where Peter Wilks had lived, the street in front of it was full of people. There were three orphaned girls standing in the doorway, all of them mourning the death of their father.

It's true. Uncle Harvey is here with Uncle William!

Those three girls hadn't seen their uncles in such a long time that they didn't know what they really looked like.

Uncle Harvey! We're so glad you could come. Father wanted to see you so much before he died.

Alas, the trip from England took too long. Words cannot describe the grief I feel today.

They were young. Mary Jane was nineteen, Susan was fifteen, and Joanna was only fourteen. None of them had come across tricksters like the duke and the king before.

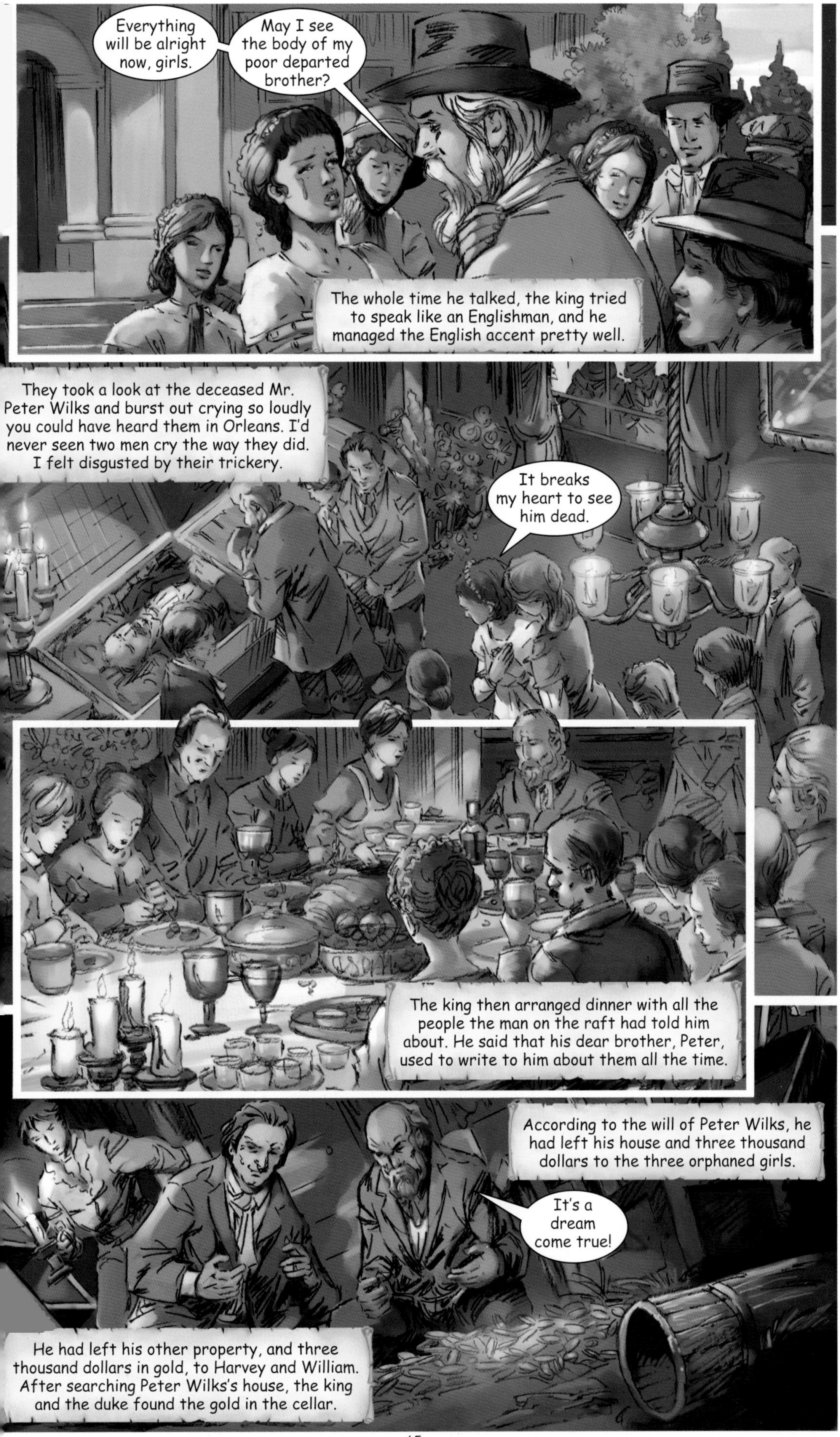
Everything will be alright now, girls.
May I see the body of my poor departed brother?
The whole time he talked, the king tried to speak like an Englishman, and he managed the English accent pretty well.
They took a look at the deceased Mr. Peter Wilks and burst out crying so loudly you could have heard them in Orleans. I'd never seen two men cry the way they did. I felt disgusted by their trickery.
It breaks my heart to see him dead.
The king then arranged dinner with all the people the man on the raft had told him about. He said that his dear brother, Peter, used to write to him about them all the time.
According to the will of Peter Wilks, he had left his house and three thousand dollars to the three orphaned girls.
It's a dream come true!
He had left his other property, and three thousand dollars in gold, to Harvey and William. After searching Peter Wilks's house, the king and the duke found the gold in the cellar.

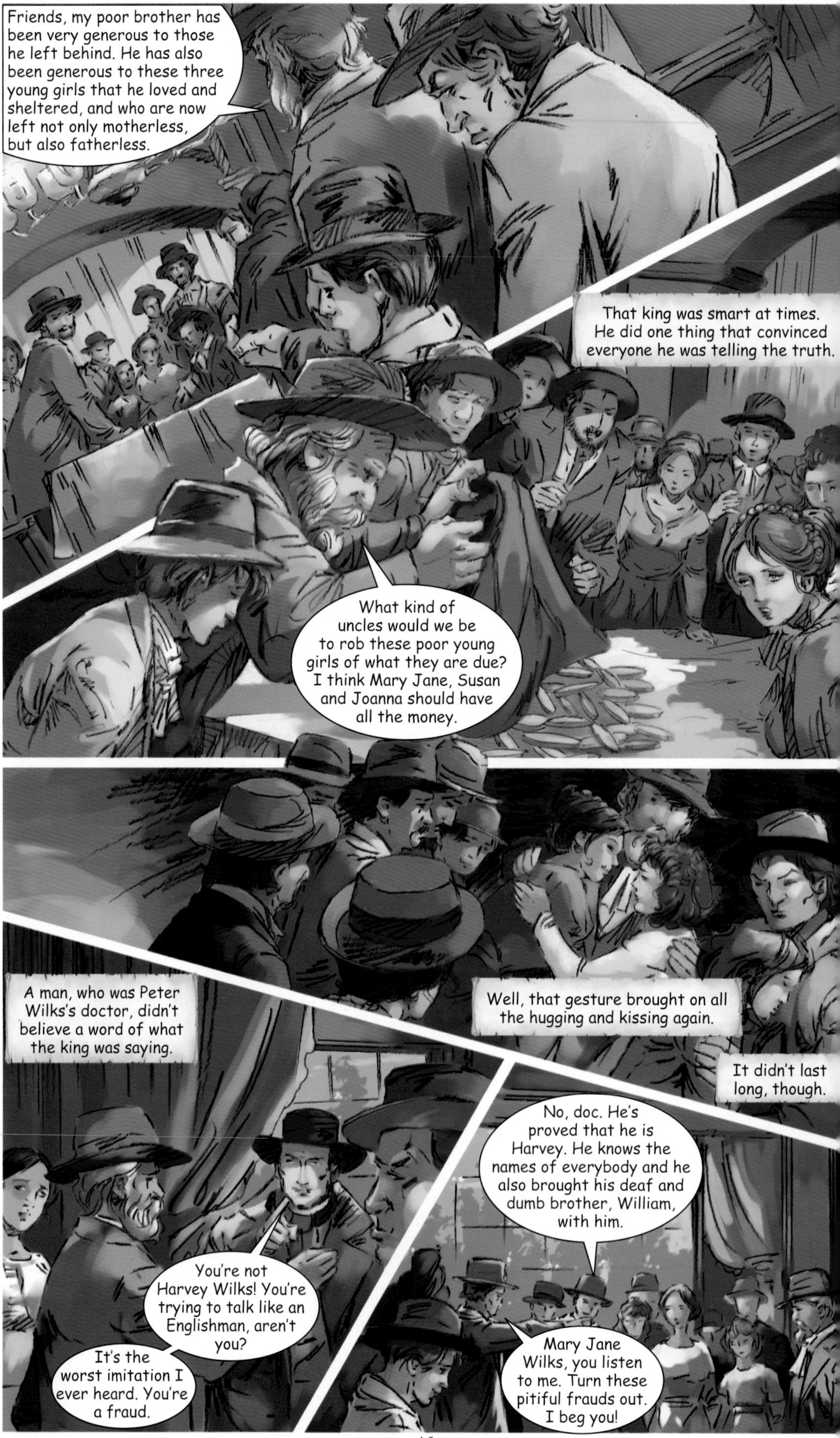
Friends, my poor brother has been very generous to those he left behind. He has also been generous to these three young girls that he loved and sheltered, and who are now left not only motherless, but also fatherless.
That king was smart at times. He did one thing that convinced everyone he was telling the truth.
What kind of uncles would we be to rob these poor young girls of what they are due? I think Mary Jane, Susan and Joanna should have all the money.
Well, that gesture brought on all the hugging and kissing again.
It didn't last long, though.
A man, who was Peter Wilks's doctor, didn't believe a word of what the king was saying.
You're not Harvey Wilks! You're trying to talk like an Englishman, aren't you?
It's the worst imitation I ever heard. You're a fraud.
No, doc. He's proved that he is Harvey. He knows the names of everybody and he also brought his deaf and dumb brother, William, with him.
Mary Jane Wilks, you listen to me. Turn these pitiful frauds out. I beg you!

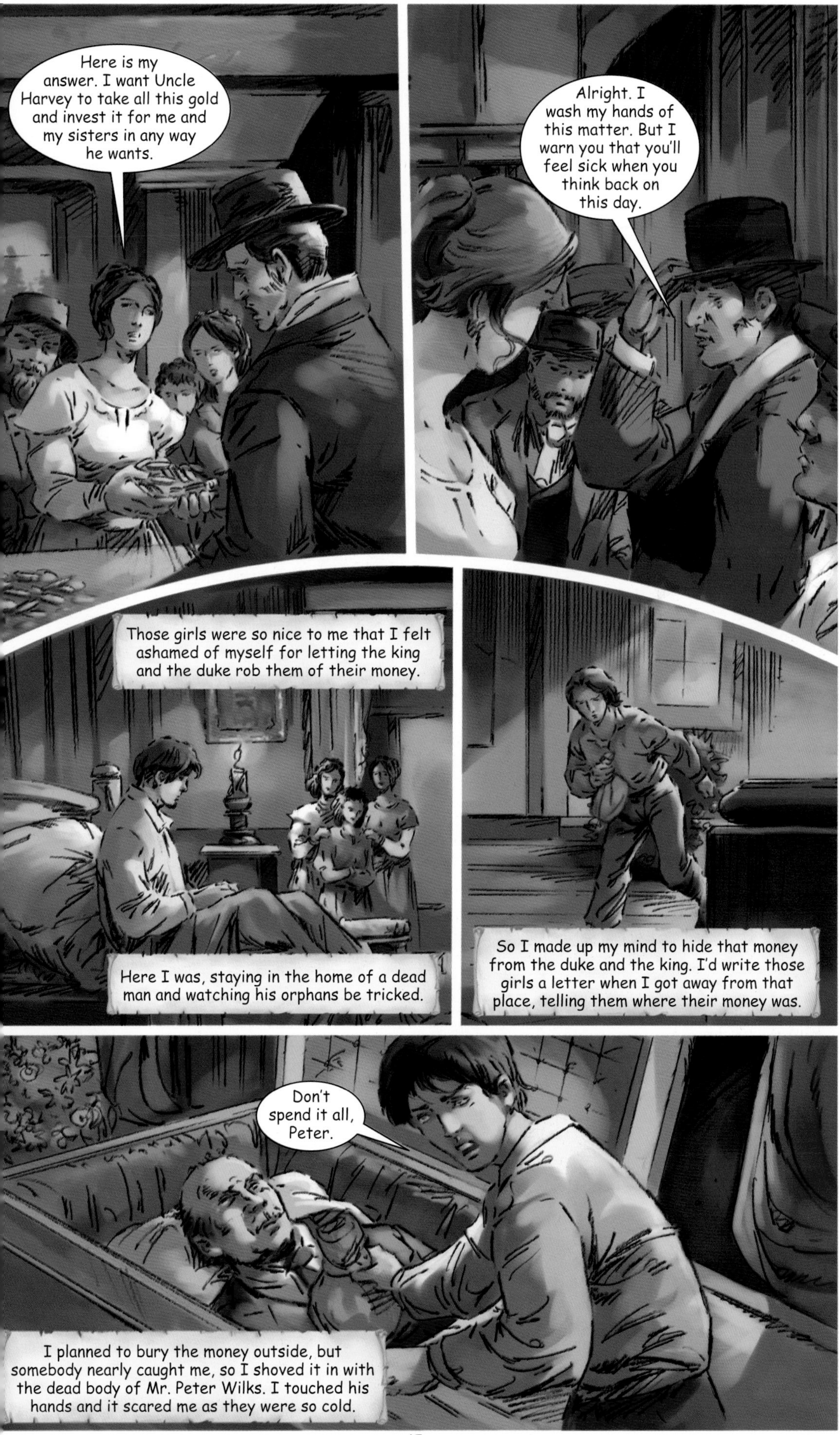
Here is my answer. I want Uncle Harvey to take all this gold and invest it for me and my sisters in any way he wants.
Alright. I wash my hands of this matter. But I warn you that you'll feel sick when you think back on this day.
Those girls were so nice to me that I felt ashamed of myself for letting the king and the duke rob them of their money.
Here I was, staying in the home of a dead man and watching his orphans be tricked.
So I made up my mind to hide that money from the duke and the king. I'd write those girls a letter when I got away from that place, telling them where their money was.
Don't spend it all, Peter.
I planned to bury the money outside, but somebody nearly caught me, so I shoved it in with the dead body of Mr. Peter Wilks. I touched his hands and it scared me as they were so cold.

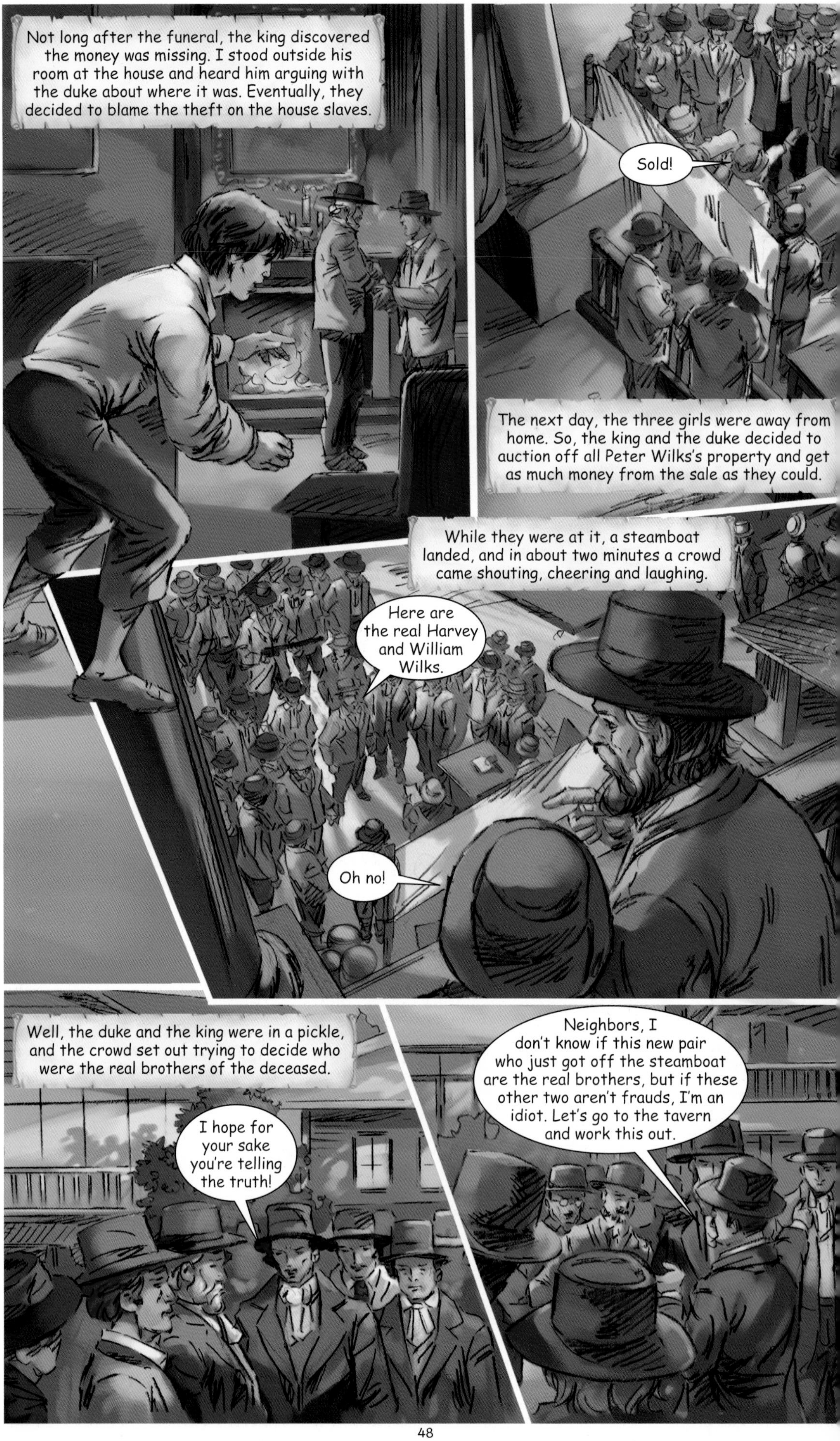
Not long after the funeral, the king discovered the money was missing. I stood outside his room at the house and heard him arguing with the duke about where it was. Eventually, they decided to blame the theft on the house slaves.
Sold!
The next day, the three girls were away from home. So, the king and the duke decided to auction off all Peter Wilks's property and get as much money from the sale as they could.
While they were at it, a steamboat landed, and in about two minutes a crowd came shouting, cheering and laughing.
Here are the real Harvey and William Wilks.
Oh no!
Well, the duke and the king were in a pickle, and the crowd set out trying to decide who were the real brothers of the deceased.
I hope for your sake you're telling the truth!
Neighbors, I don't know if this new pair who just got off the steamboat are the real brothers, but if these other two aren't frauds, I'm an idiot. Let's go to the tavern and work this out.

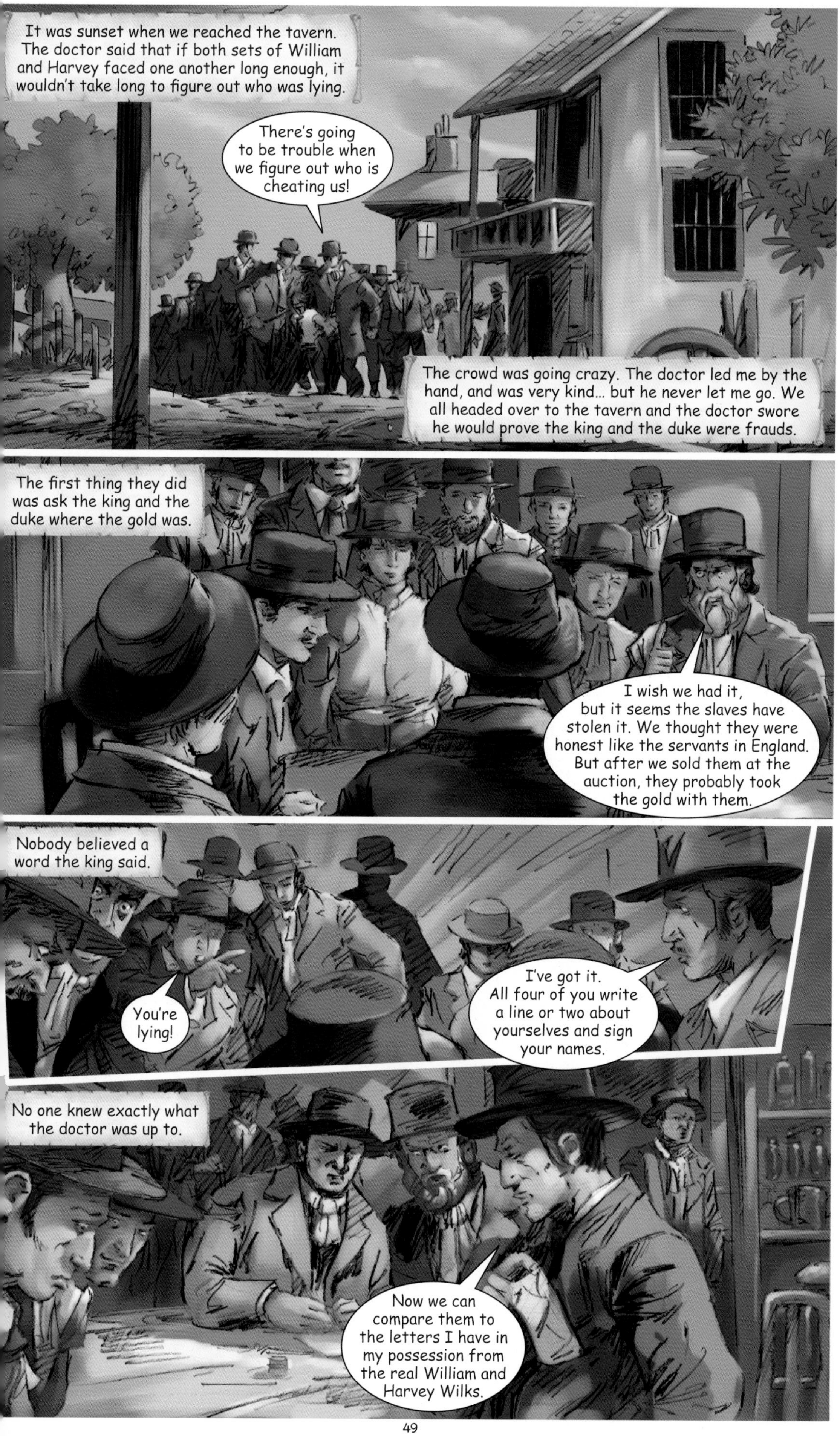
It was sunset when we reached the tavern. The doctor said that if both sets of William and Harvey faced one another long enough, it wouldn't take long to figure out who was lying.
There's going to be trouble when we figure out who is cheating us!
The crowd was going crazy. The doctor led me by the hand, and was very kind... but he never let me go. We all headed over to the tavern and the doctor swore he would prove the king and the duke were frauds.
The first thing they did was ask the king and the duke where the gold was.
I wish we had it, but it seems the slaves have stolen it. We thought they were honest like the servants in England. But after we sold them at the auction, they probably took the gold with them.
Nobody believed a word the king said.
You're lying!
I've got it. All four of you write a line or two about yourselves and sign your names.
No one knew exactly what the doctor was up to.
Now we can compare them to the letters I have in my possession from the real William and Harvey Wilks.

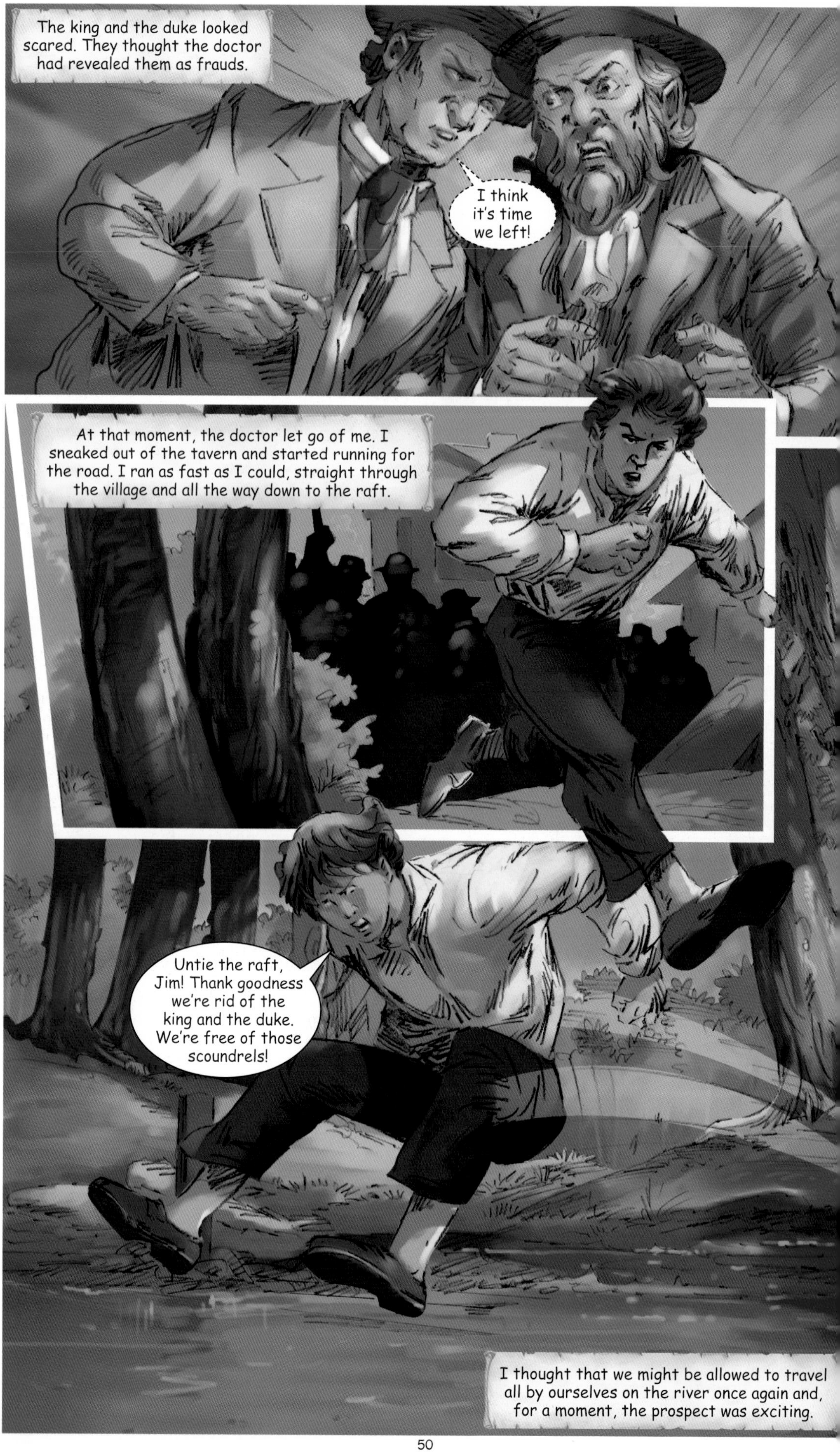
The king and the duke looked scared. They thought the doctor had revealed them as frauds.
I think it's time we left!
At that moment, the doctor let go of me. I sneaked out of the tavern and started running for the road. I ran as fast as I could, straight through the village and all the way down to the raft.
Untie the raft, Jim! Thank goodness we're rid of the king and the duke. We're free of those scoundrels!
I thought that we might be allowed to travel all by ourselves on the river once again and, for a moment, the prospect was exciting.

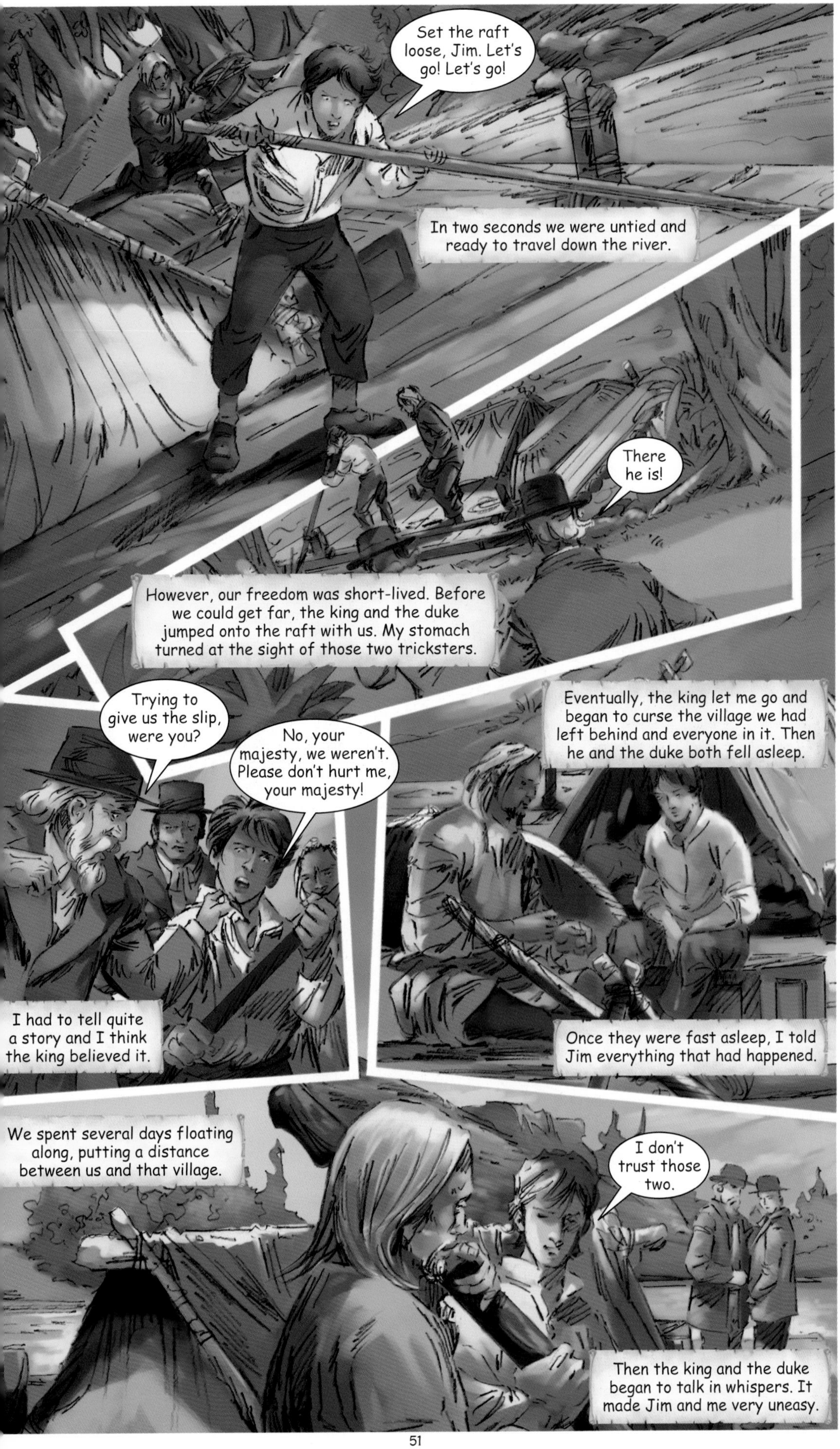
Set the raft loose, Jim. Let's go! Let's go!
In two seconds we were untied and ready to travel down the river.
There he is!
However, our freedom was short-lived. Before we could get far, the king and the duke jumped onto the raft with us. My stomach turned at the sight of those two tricksters.
Trying to give us the slip, were you?
No, your majesty, we weren't. Please don't hurt me, your majesty!
I had to tell quite a story and I think the king believed it.
Eventually, the king let me go and began to curse the village we had left behind and everyone in it. Then he and the duke both fell asleep.
Once they were fast asleep, I told Jim everything that had happened.
We spent several days floating along, putting a distance between us and that village.
I don't trust those two.
Then the king and the duke began to talk in whispers. It made Jim and me very uneasy.

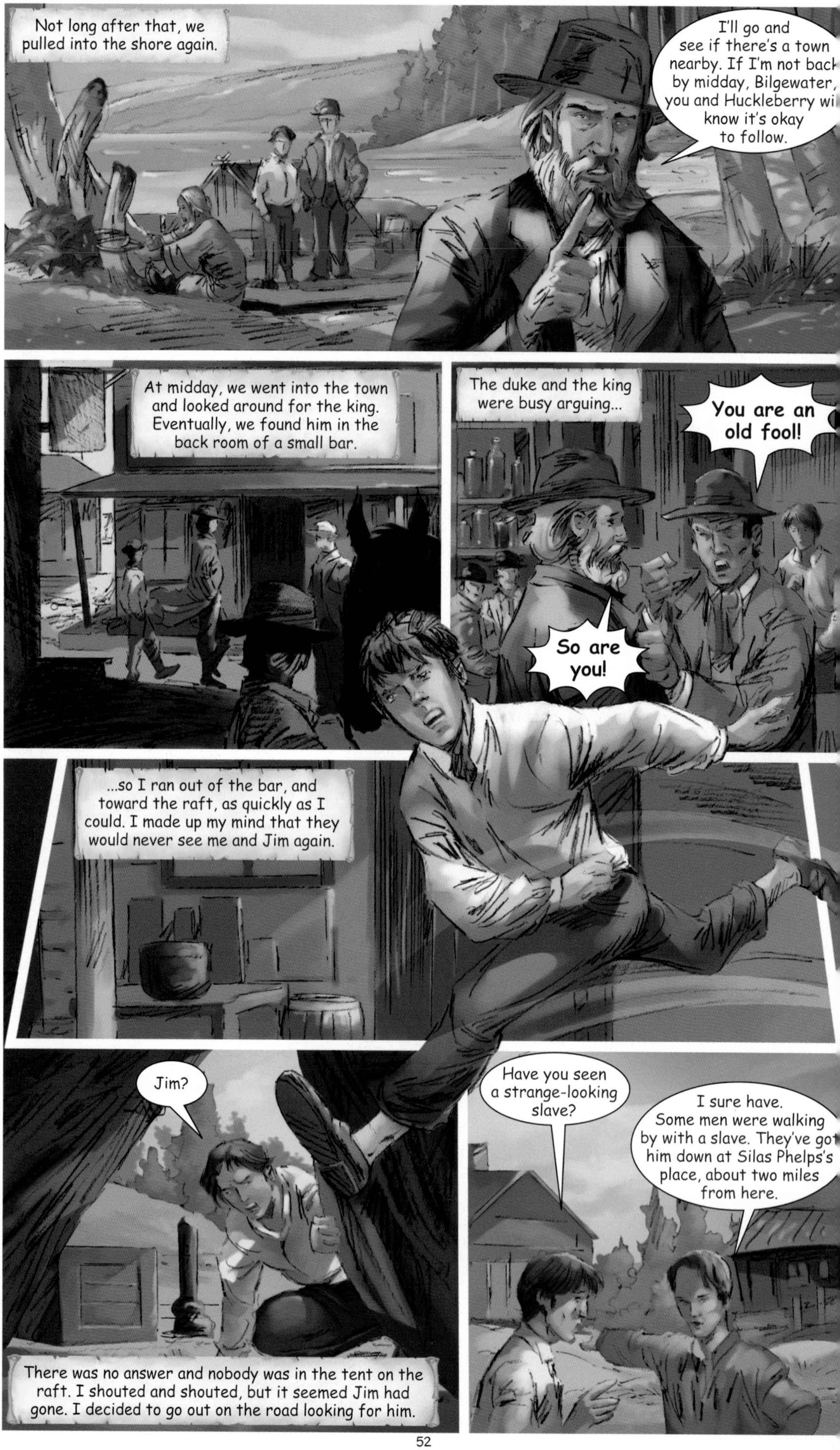

Not long after that, we pulled into the shore again.
I'll go and see if there's a town nearby. If I'm not back by midday, Bilgewater, you and Huckleberry will know it's okay to follow.
At midday, we went into the town and looked around for the king. Eventually, we found him in the back room of a small bar.
The duke and the king were busy arguing...
You are an old fool!
So are you!
...so I ran out of the bar, and toward the raft, as quickly as I could. I made up my mind that they would never see me and Jim again.
Jim?
There was no answer and nobody was in the tent on the raft. I shouted and shouted, but it seemed Jim had gone. I decided to go out on the road looking for him.
Have you seen a strange-looking slave?
I sure have. Some men were walking by with a slave. They've got him down at Silas Phelps's place, about two miles from here.

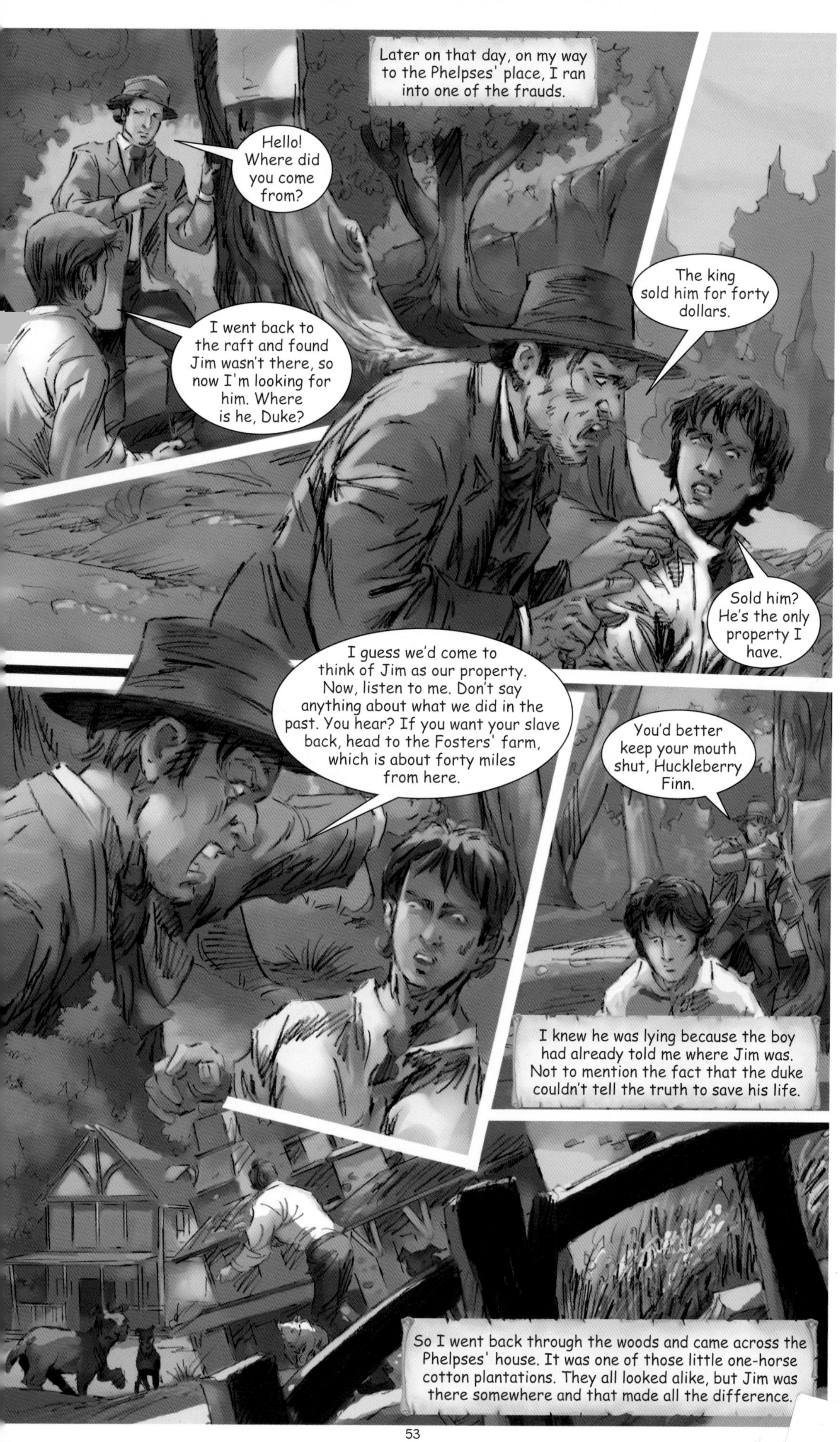
Later on that day, on my way to the Phelpses' place, I ran into one of the frauds.
Hello! Where did you come from?
I went back to the raft and found Jim wasn't there, so now I'm looking for him. Where is he, Duke?
The king sold him for forty dollars.
Sold him? He's the only property I have.
I guess we'd come to think of Jim as our property. Now, listen to me. Don't say anything about what we did in the past. You hear? If you want your slave back, head to the Fosters' farm, which is about forty miles from here.
You'd better keep your mouth shut, Huckleberry Finn.
I knew he was lying because the boy had already told me where Jim was. Not to mention the fact that the duke couldn't tell the truth to save his life.
So I went back through the woods and came across the Phelpses' house. It was one of those little one-horse cotton plantations. They all looked alike, but Jim was there somewhere and that made all the difference.

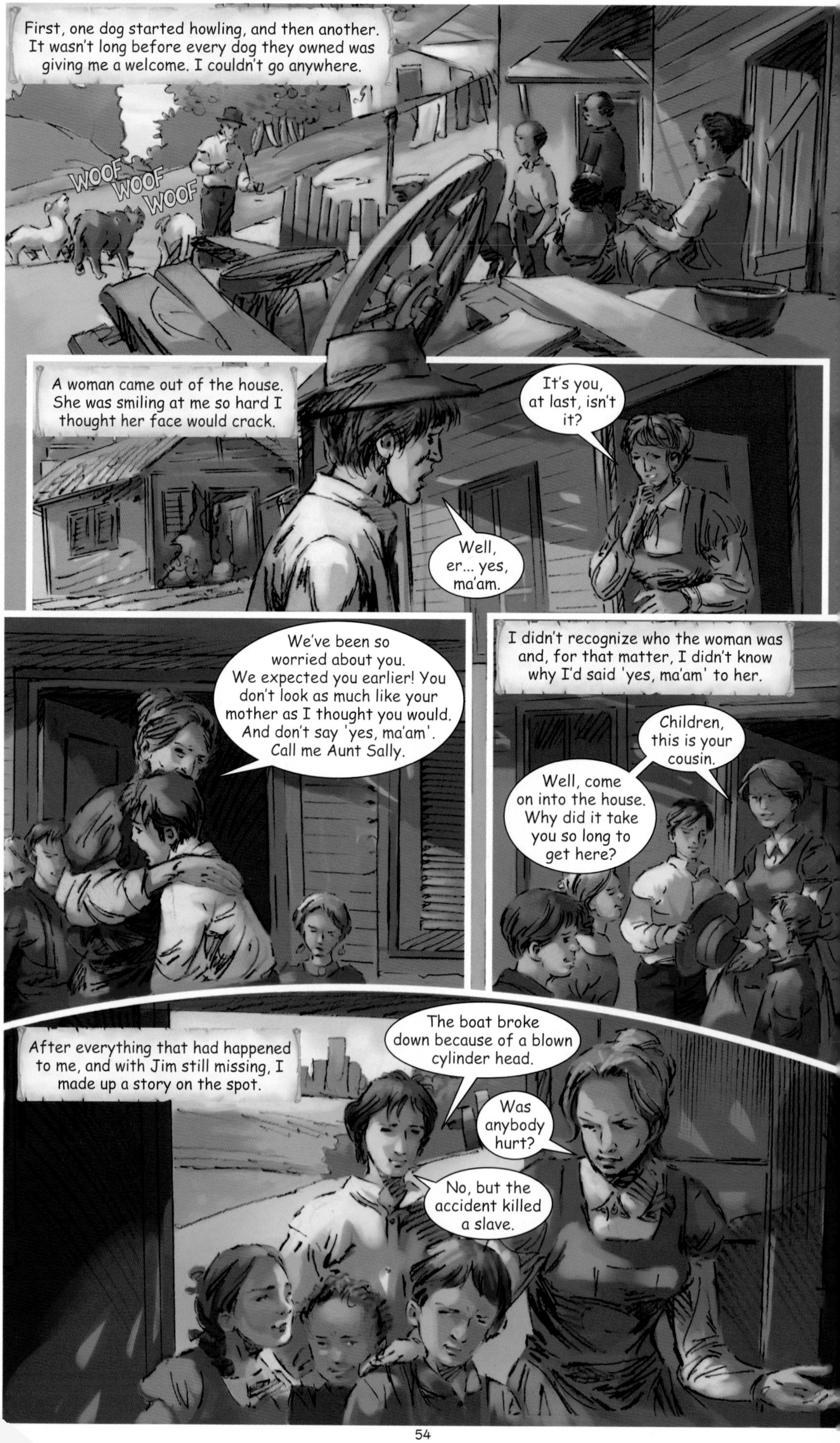
First, one dog started howling, and then another. It wasn't long before every dog they owned was giving me a welcome. I couldn't go anywhere.
WOOF
WOOF
WOOF
A woman came out of the house. She was smiling at me so hard I thought her face would crack.
It's you, at last, isn't it?
Well, er... yes, ma'am.
We've been so worried about you. We expected you earlier! You don't look as much like your mother as I thought you would. And don't say 'yes, ma'am'. Call me Aunt Sally.
I didn't recognize who the woman was and, for that matter, I didn't know why I'd said 'yes, ma'am' to her.
Children, this is your cousin.
Well, come on into the house. Why did it take you so long to get here?
After everything that had happened to me, and with Jim still missing, I made up a story on the spot.
The boat broke down because of a blown cylinder head.
Was anybody hurt?
No, but the accident killed a slave.

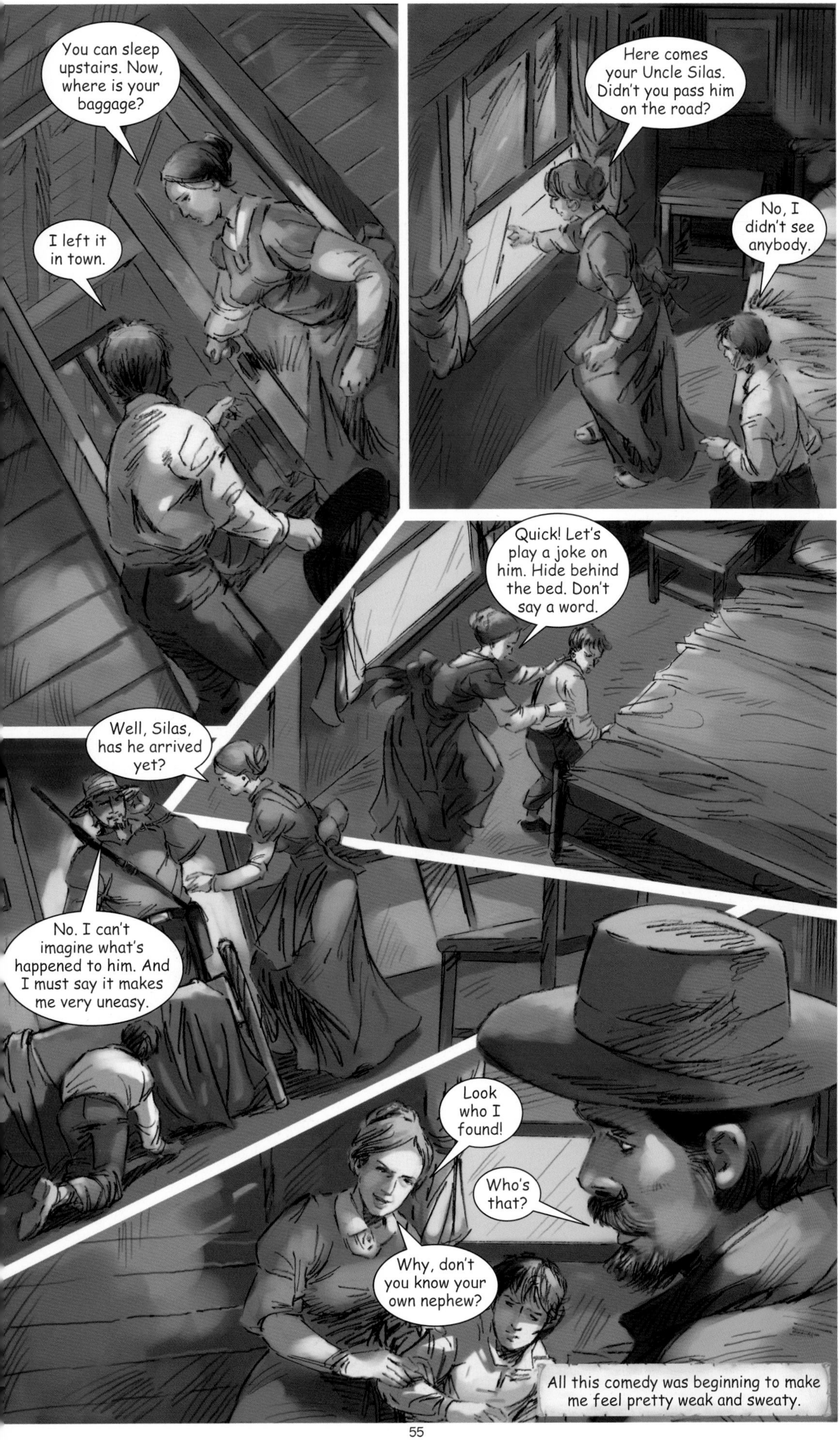

You can sleep upstairs. Now, where is your baggage?
I left it in town.
Here comes your Uncle Silas. Didn't you pass him on the road?
No, I didn't see anybody.
Quick! Let's play a joke on him. Hide behind the bed. Don't say a word.
Well, Silas, has he arrived yet?
No. I can't imagine what's happened to him. And I must say it makes me very uneasy.
Look who I found!
Who's that?
Why, don't you know your own nephew?
All this comedy was beginning to make me feel pretty weak and sweaty.

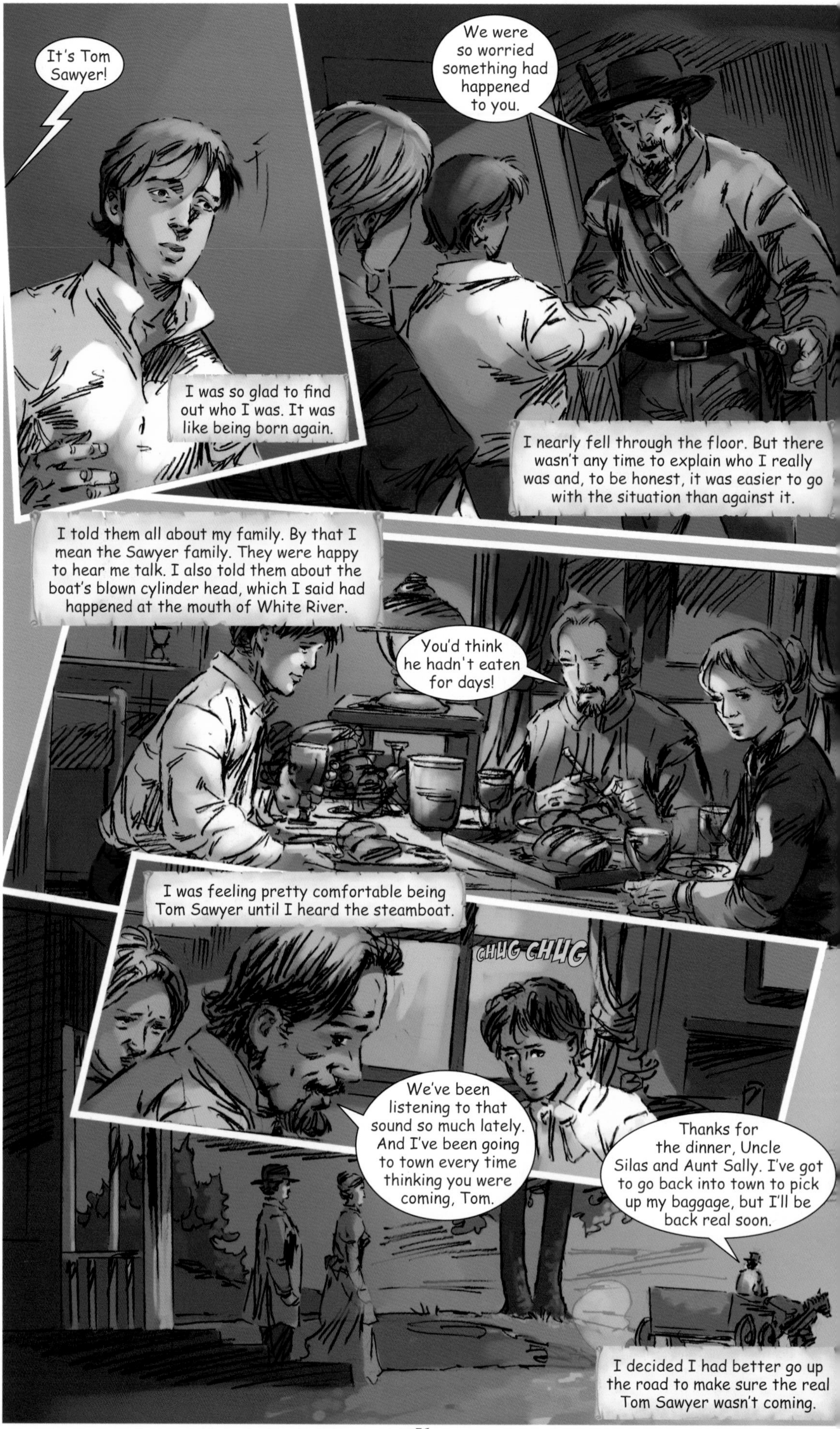
It's Tom Sawyer!
I was so glad to find out who I was. It was like being born again.
We were so worried something had happened to you.
I nearly fell through the floor. But there wasn't any time to explain who I really was and, to be honest, it was easier to go with the situation than against it.
I told them all about my family. By that I mean the Sawyer family. They were happy to hear me talk. I also told them about the boat's blown cylinder head, which I said had happened at the mouth of White River.
You'd think he hadn't eaten for days!
I was feeling pretty comfortable being Tom Sawyer until I heard the steamboat.
CHUG CHUG
We've been listening to that sound so much lately. And I've been going to town every time thinking you were coming, Tom.
Thanks for the dinner, Uncle Silas and Aunt Sally. I've got to go back into town to pick up my baggage, but I'll be back real soon.
I decided I had better go up the road to make sure the real Tom Sawyer wasn't coming.

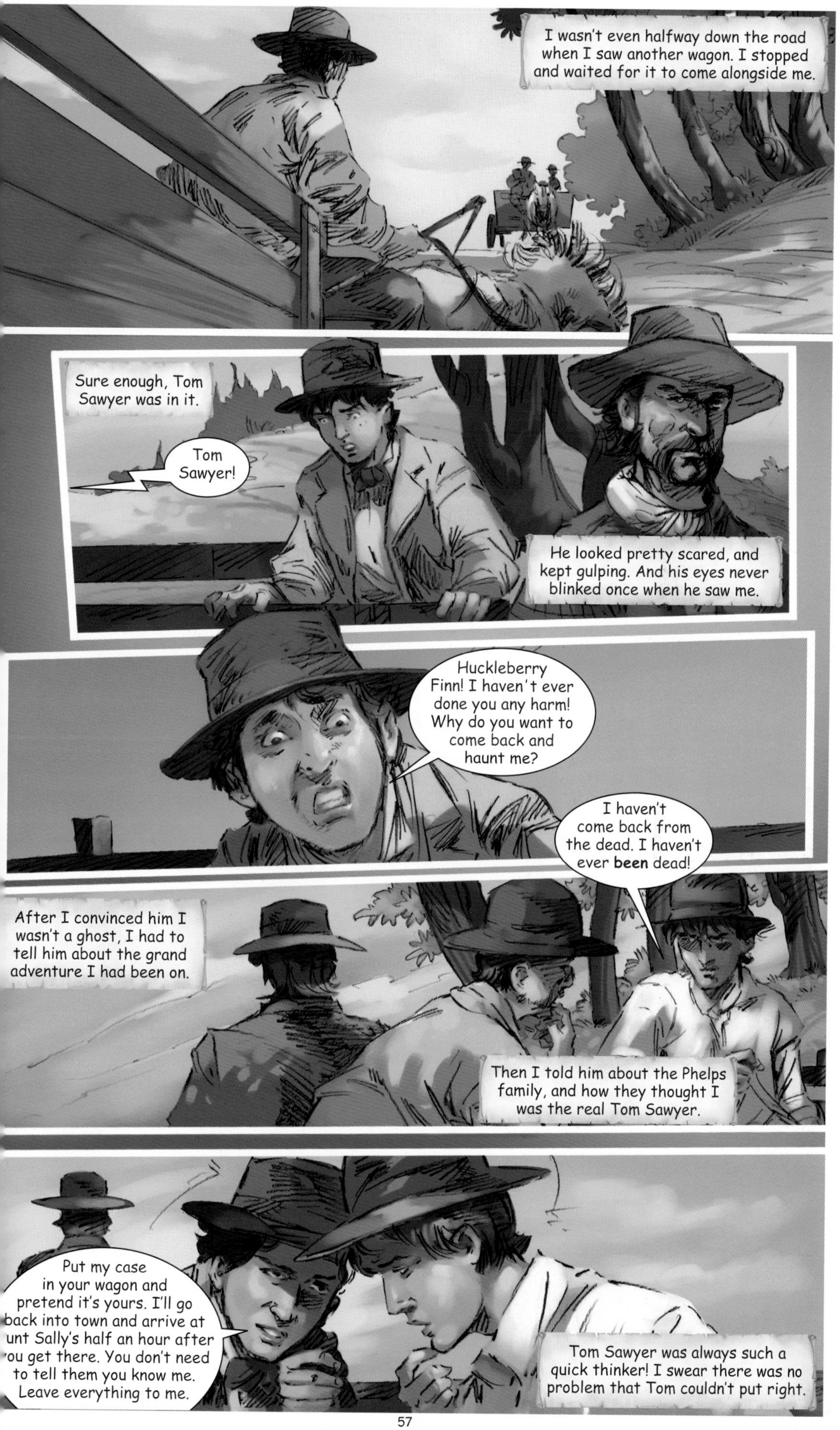

I wasn't even halfway down the road when I saw another wagon. I stopped and waited for it to come alongside me.
Sure enough, Tom Sawyer was in it.
Tom Sawyer!
He looked pretty scared, and kept gulping. And his eyes never blinked once when he saw me.
Huckleberry Finn! I haven't ever done you any harm! Why do you want to come back and haunt me?
I haven't come back from the dead. I haven't ever **been** dead!
After I convinced him I wasn't a ghost, I had to tell him about the grand adventure I had been on.
Then I told him about the Phelps family, and how they thought I was the real Tom Sawyer.
Put my case in your wagon and pretend it's yours. I'll go back into town and arrive at unt Sally's half an hour after ou get there. You don't need to tell them you know me. Leave everything to me.
Tom Sawyer was always such a quick thinker! I swear there was no problem that Tom couldn't put right.

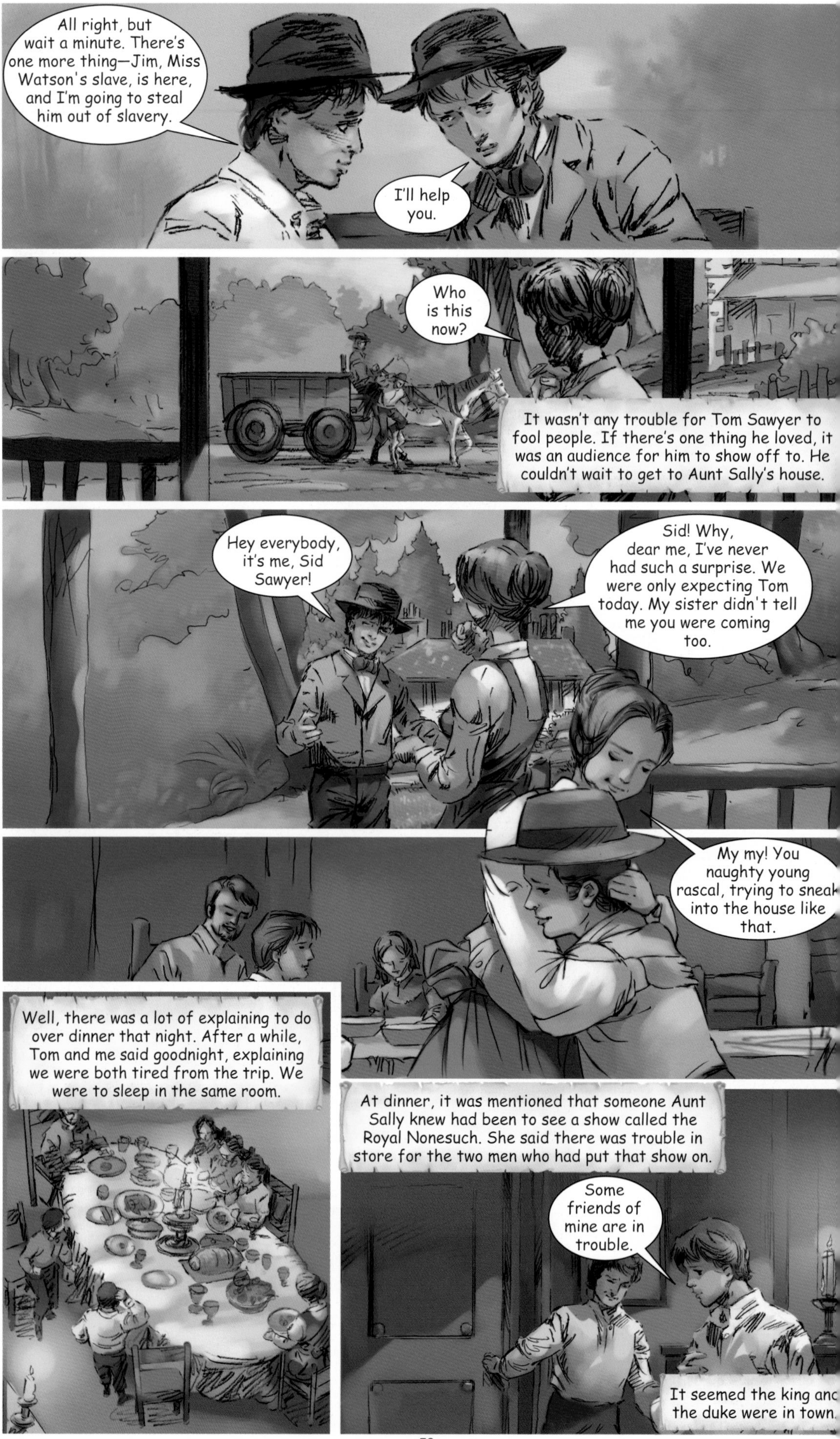
All right, but wait a minute. There's one more thing—Jim, Miss Watson's slave, is here, and I'm going to steal him out of slavery.
I'll help you.
Who is this now?
It wasn't any trouble for Tom Sawyer to fool people. If there's one thing he loved, it was an audience for him to show off to. He couldn't wait to get to Aunt Sally's house.
Hey everybody, it's me, Sid Sawyer!
Sid! Why, dear me, I've never had such a surprise. We were only expecting Tom today. My sister didn't tell me you were coming too.
My my! You naughty young rascal, trying to sneak into the house like that.
Well, there was a lot of explaining to do over dinner that night. After a while, Tom and me said goodnight, explaining we were both tired from the trip. We were to sleep in the same room.
At dinner, it was mentioned that someone Aunt Sally knew had been to see a show called the Royal Nonesuch. She said there was trouble in store for the two men who had put that show on.
Some friends of mine are in trouble.
It seemed the king and the duke were in town.

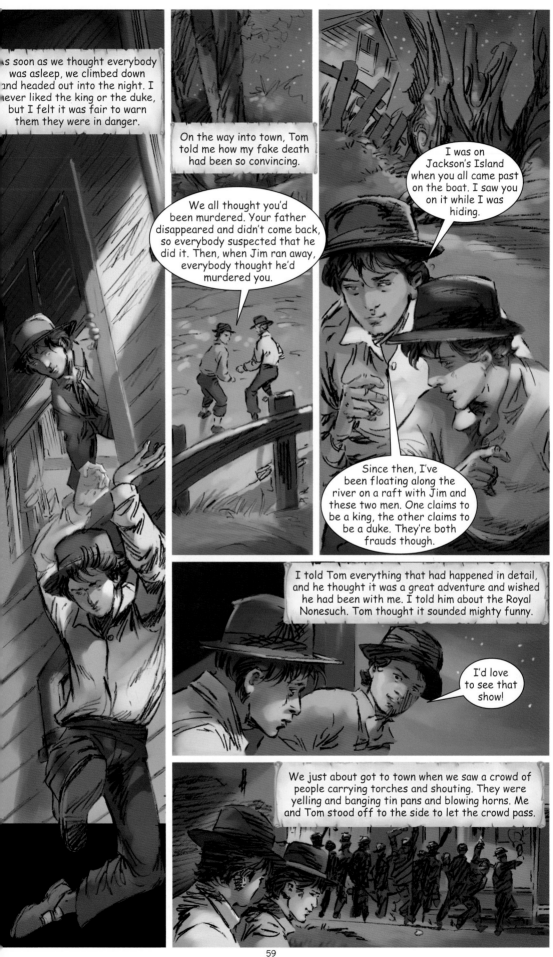

As soon as we thought everybody was asleep, we climbed down and headed out into the night. I never liked the king or the duke, but I felt it was fair to warn them they were in danger.

On the way into town, Tom told me how my fake death had been so convincing.

We all thought you'd been murdered. Your father disappeared and didn't come back, so everybody suspected that he did it. Then, when Jim ran away, everybody thought he'd murdered you.

I was on Jackson's Island when you all came past on the boat. I saw you on it while I was hiding.

Since then, I've been floating along the river on a raft with Jim and these two men. One claims to be a king, the other claims to be a duke. They're both frauds though.

I told Tom everything that had happened in detail, and he thought it was a great adventure and wished he had been with me. I told him about the Royal Nonesuch. Tom thought it sounded mighty funny.

I'd love to see that show!

We just about got to town when we saw a crowd of people carrying torches and shouting. They were yelling and banging tin pans and blowing horns. Me and Tom stood off to the side to let the crowd pass.

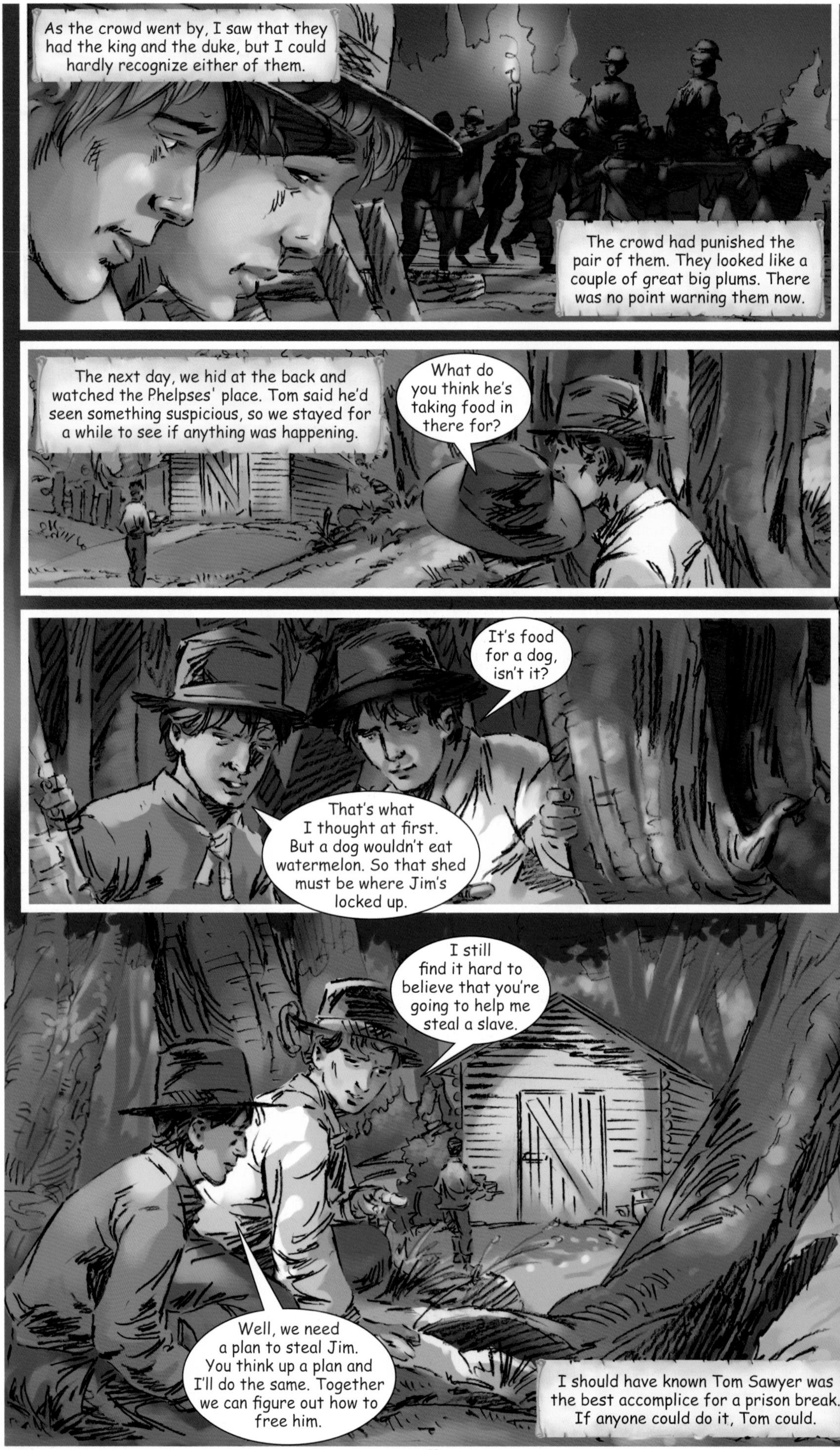

As the crowd went by, I saw that they had the king and the duke, but I could hardly recognize either of them.
The crowd had punished the pair of them. They looked like a couple of great big plums. There was no point warning them now.
The next day, we hid at the back and watched the Phelpses' place. Tom said he'd seen something suspicious, so we stayed for a while to see if anything was happening.
What do you think he's taking food in there for?
It's food for a dog, isn't it?
That's what I thought at first. But a dog wouldn't eat watermelon. So that shed must be where Jim's locked up.
I still find it hard to believe that you're going to help me steal a slave.
Well, we need a plan to steal Jim. You think up a plan and I'll do the same. Together we can figure out how to free him.
I should have known Tom Sawyer was the best accomplice for a prison break. If anyone could do it, Tom could.

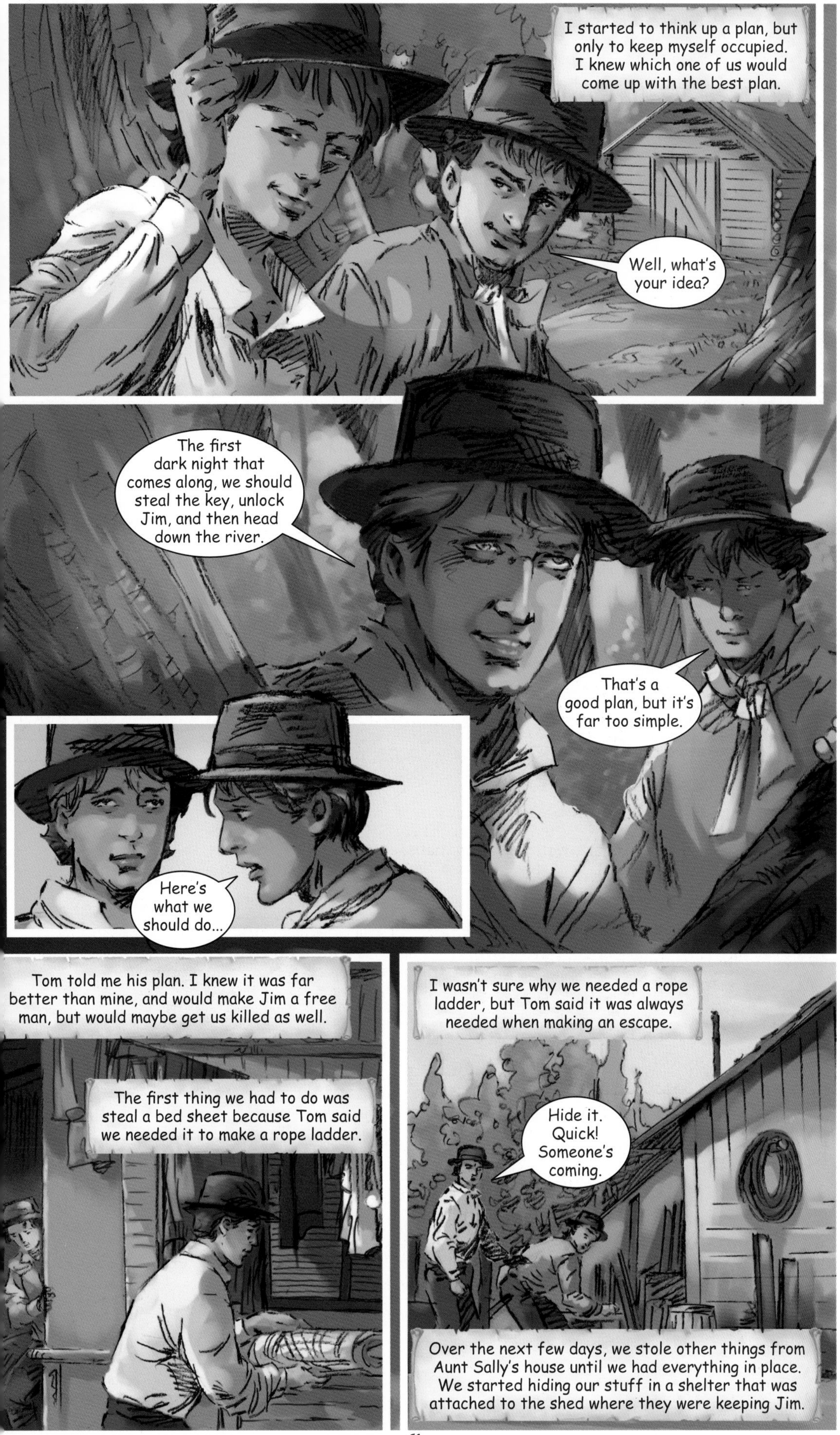
I started to think up a plan, but only to keep myself occupied. I knew which one of us would come up with the best plan.
Well, what's your idea?
The first dark night that comes along, we should steal the key, unlock Jim, and then head down the river.
That's a good plan, but it's far too simple.
Here's what we should do...
Tom told me his plan. I knew it was far better than mine, and would make Jim a free man, but would maybe get us killed as well.
The first thing we had to do was steal a bed sheet because Tom said we needed it to make a rope ladder.
I wasn't sure why we needed a rope ladder, but Tom said it was always needed when making an escape.
Hide it. Quick! Someone's coming.
Over the next few days, we stole other things from Aunt Sally's house until we had everything in place. We started hiding our stuff in a shelter that was attached to the shed where they were keeping Jim.

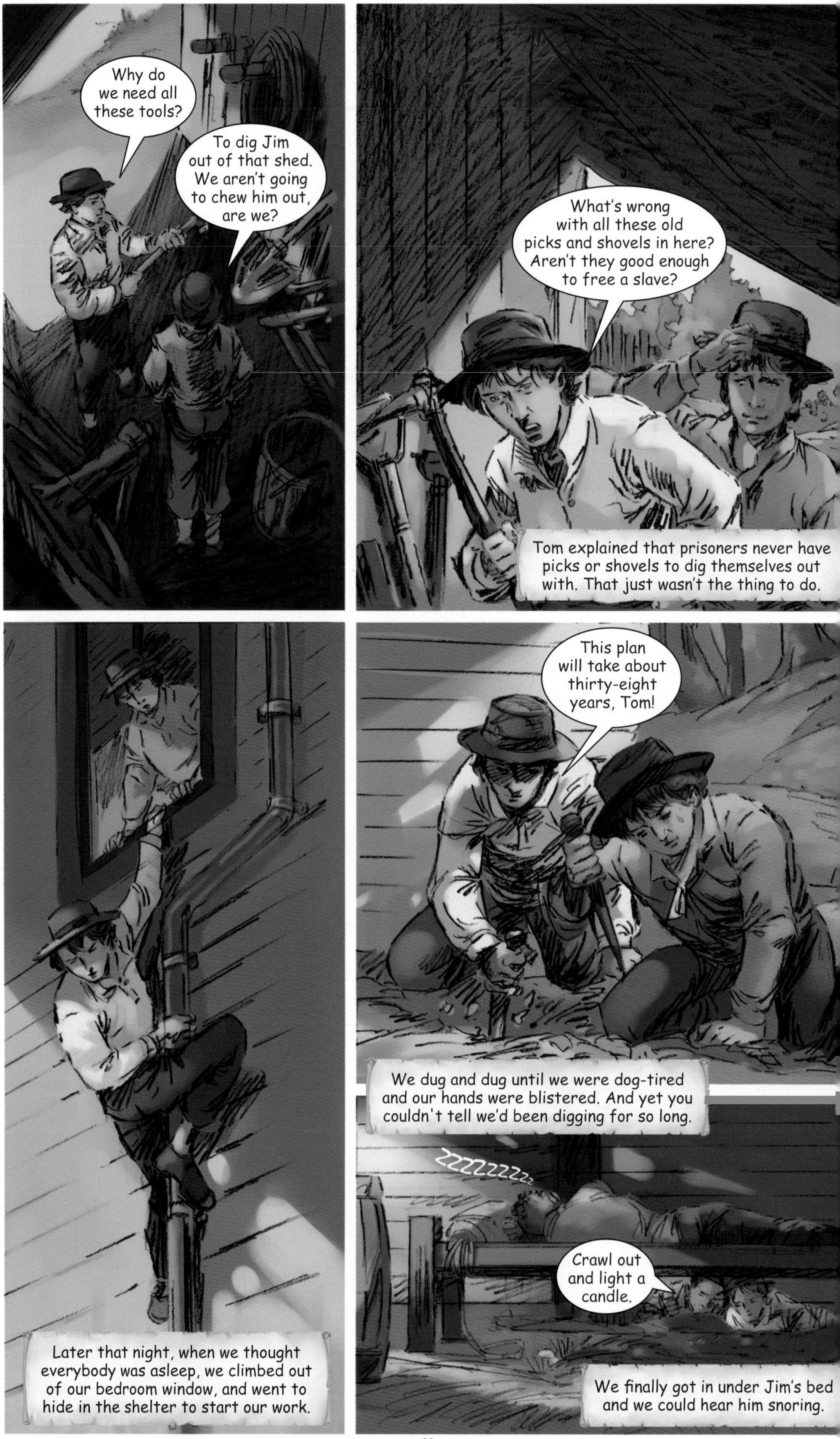
Why do we need all these tools?
To dig Jim out of that shed. We aren't going to chew him out, are we?
What's wrong with all these old picks and shovels in here? Aren't they good enough to free a slave?
Tom explained that prisoners never have picks or shovels to dig themselves out with. That just wasn't the thing to do.
Later that night, when we thought everybody was asleep, we climbed out of our bedroom window, and went to hide in the shelter to start our work.
This plan will take about thirty-eight years, Tom!
We dug and dug until we were dog-tired and our hands were blistered. And yet you couldn't tell we'd been digging for so long.
ZZZZZZZZzz
Crawl out and light a candle.
We finally got in under Jim's bed and we could hear him snoring.

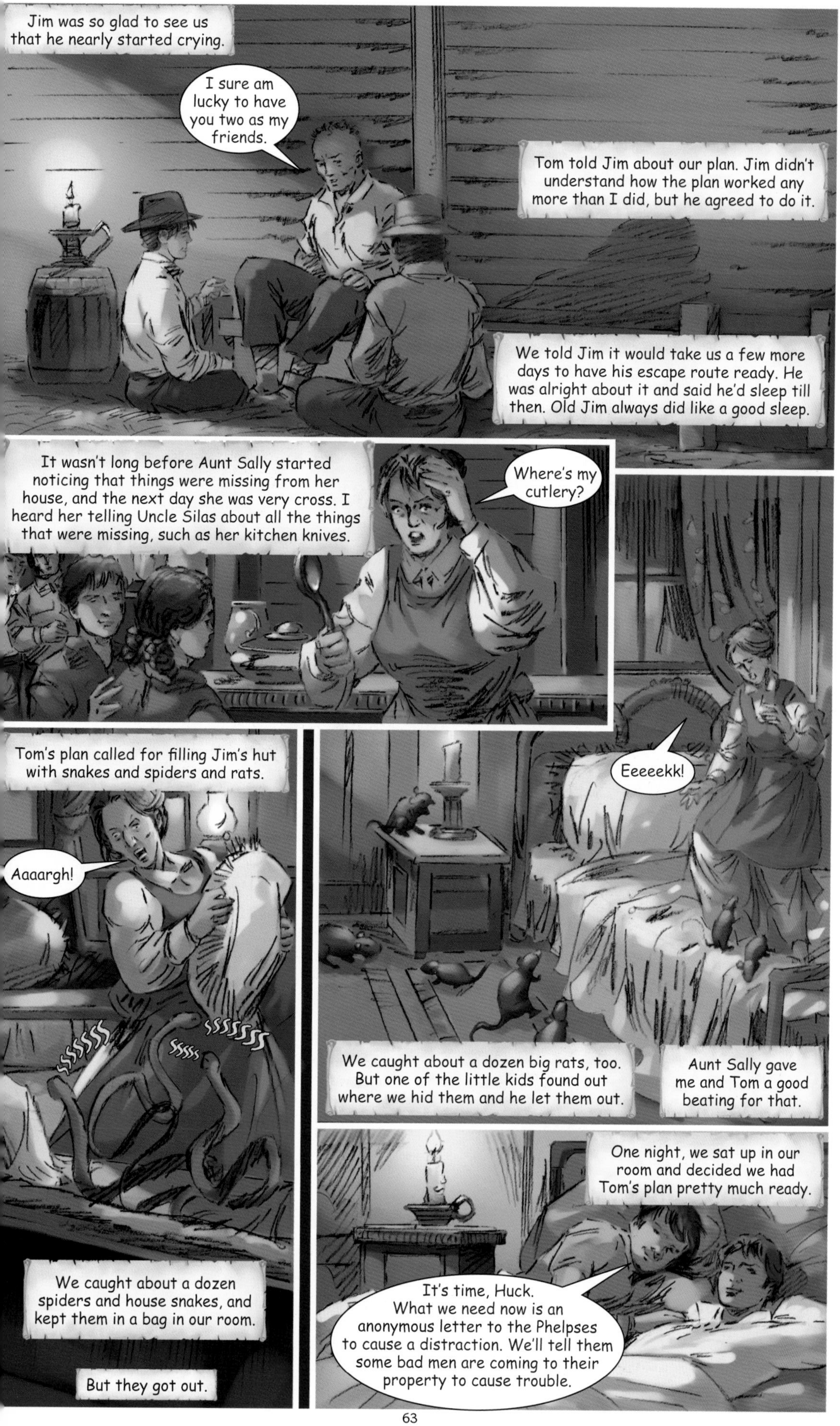
Jim was so glad to see us that he nearly started crying.
I sure am lucky to have you two as my friends.
Tom told Jim about our plan. Jim didn't understand how the plan worked any more than I did, but he agreed to do it.
We told Jim it would take us a few more days to have his escape route ready. He was alright about it and said he'd sleep till then. Old Jim always did like a good sleep.
It wasn't long before Aunt Sally started noticing that things were missing from her house, and the next day she was very cross. I heard her telling Uncle Silas about all the things that were missing, such as her kitchen knives.
Where's my cutlery?
Tom's plan called for filling Jim's hut with snakes and spiders and rats.
Aaaargh!
SSSSSSS
SSSSSSSS
SSSSS
We caught about a dozen spiders and house snakes, and kept them in a bag in our room.
But they got out.
Eeeeekk!
We caught about a dozen big rats, too. But one of the little kids found out where we hid them and he let them out.
Aunt Sally gave me and Tom a good beating for that.
One night, we sat up in our room and decided we had Tom's plan pretty much ready.
It's time, Huck. What we need now is an anonymous letter to the Phelpses to cause a distraction. We'll tell them some bad men are coming to their property to cause trouble.

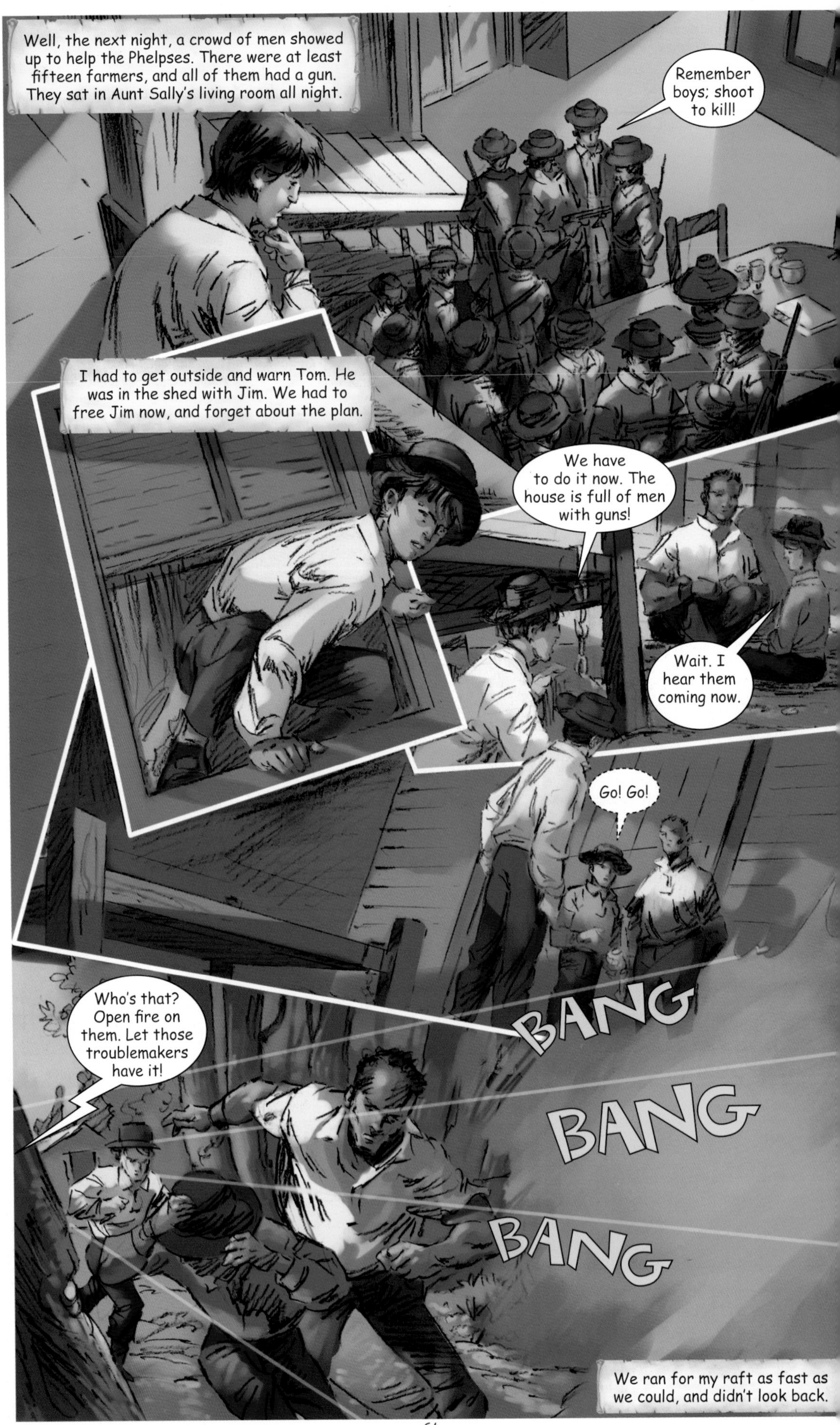

Well, the next night, a crowd of men showed up to help the Phelpses. There were at least fifteen farmers, and all of them had a gun. They sat in Aunt Sally's living room all night.
Remember boys; shoot to kill!
I had to get outside and warn Tom. He was in the shed with Jim. We had to free Jim now, and forget about the plan.
We have to do it now. The house is full of men with guns!
Wait. I hear them coming now.
Go! Go!
Who's that? Open fire on them. Let those troublemakers have it!
BANG
BANG
BANG
We ran for my raft as fast as we could, and didn't look back.

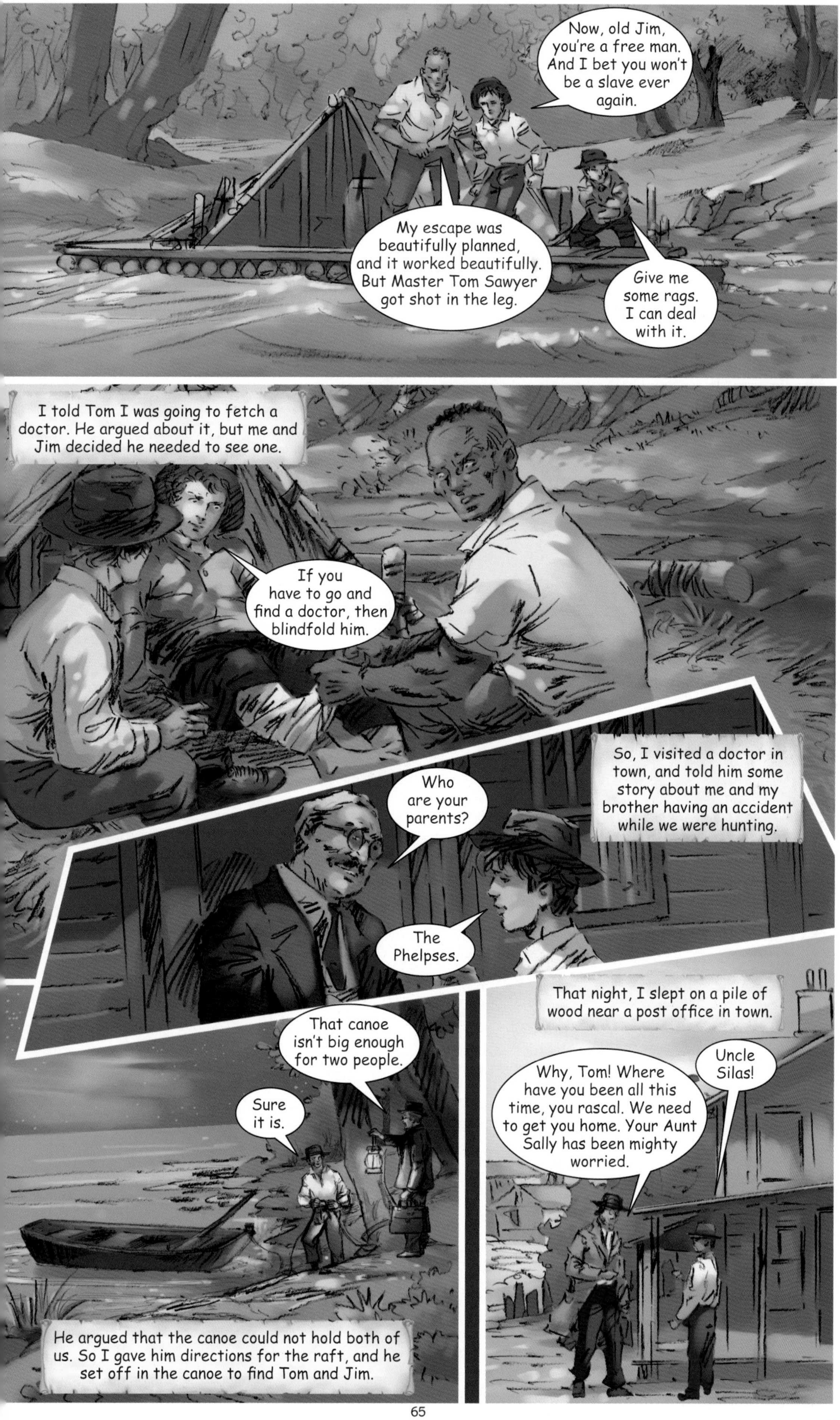
Now, old Jim, you're a free man. And I bet you won't be a slave ever again.
My escape was beautifully planned, and it worked beautifully. But Master Tom Sawyer got shot in the leg.
Give me some rags. I can deal with it.
I told Tom I was going to fetch a doctor. He argued about it, but me and Jim decided he needed to see one.
If you have to go and find a doctor, then blindfold him.
So, I visited a doctor in town, and told him some story about me and my brother having an accident while we were hunting.
Who are your parents?
The Phelpses.
That canoe isn't big enough for two people.
Sure it is.
He argued that the canoe could not hold both of us. So I gave him directions for the raft, and he set off in the canoe to find Tom and Jim.
That night, I slept on a pile of wood near a post office in town.
Why, Tom! Where have you been all this time, you rascal. We need to get you home. Your Aunt Sally has been mighty worried.
Uncle Silas!

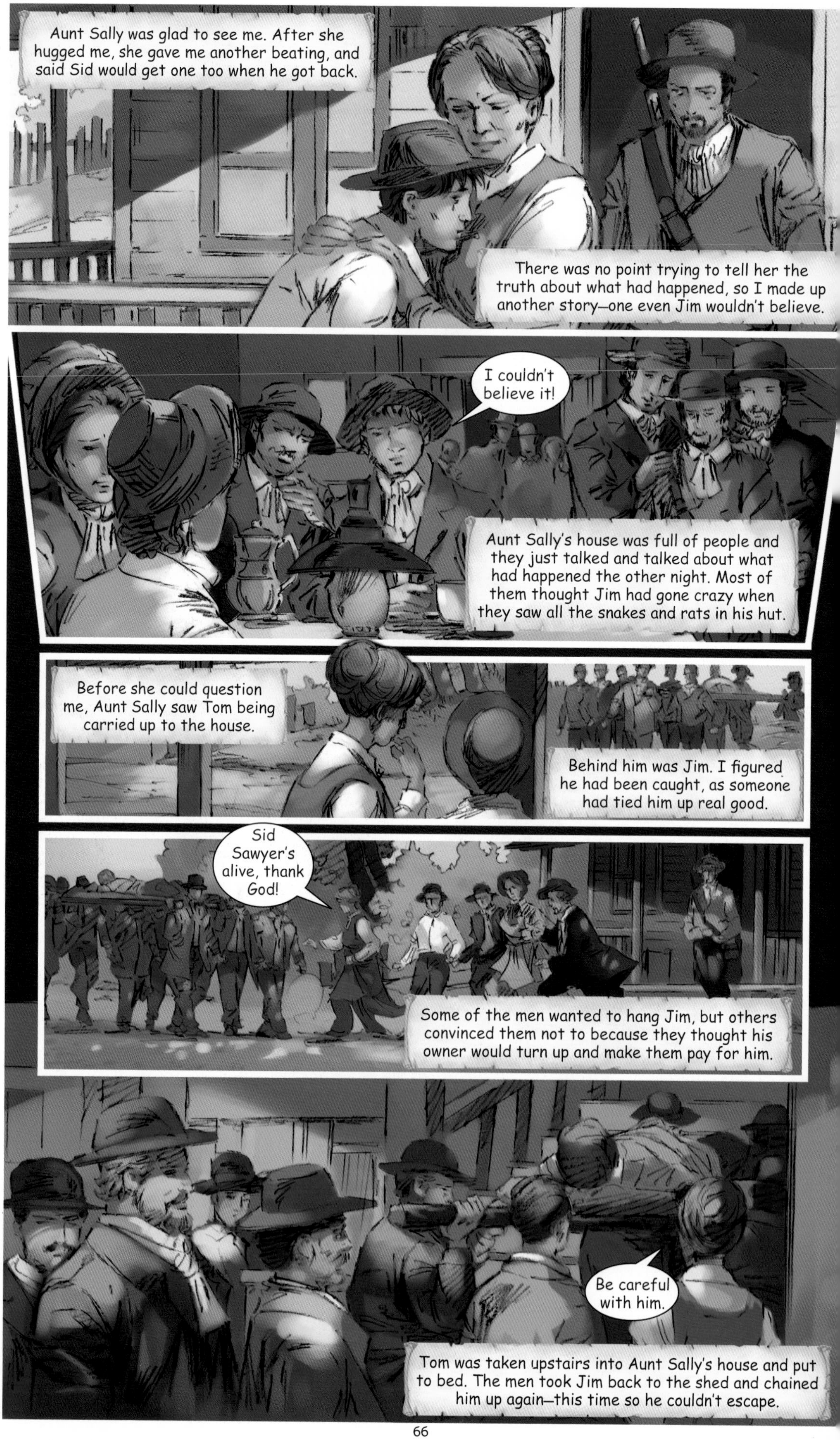
Aunt Sally was glad to see me. After she hugged me, she gave me another beating, and said Sid would get one too when he got back.
There was no point trying to tell her the truth about what had happened, so I made up another story—one even Jim wouldn't believe.
I couldn't believe it!
Aunt Sally's house was full of people and they just talked and talked about what had happened the other night. Most of them thought Jim had gone crazy when they saw all the snakes and rats in his hut.
Before she could question me, Aunt Sally saw Tom being carried up to the house.
Behind him was Jim. I figured he had been caught, as someone had tied him up real good.
Sid Sawyer's alive, thank God!
Some of the men wanted to hang Jim, but others convinced them not to because they thought his owner would turn up and make them pay for him.
Be careful with him.
Tom was taken upstairs into Aunt Sally's house and put to bed. The men took Jim back to the shed and chained him up again—this time so he couldn't escape.

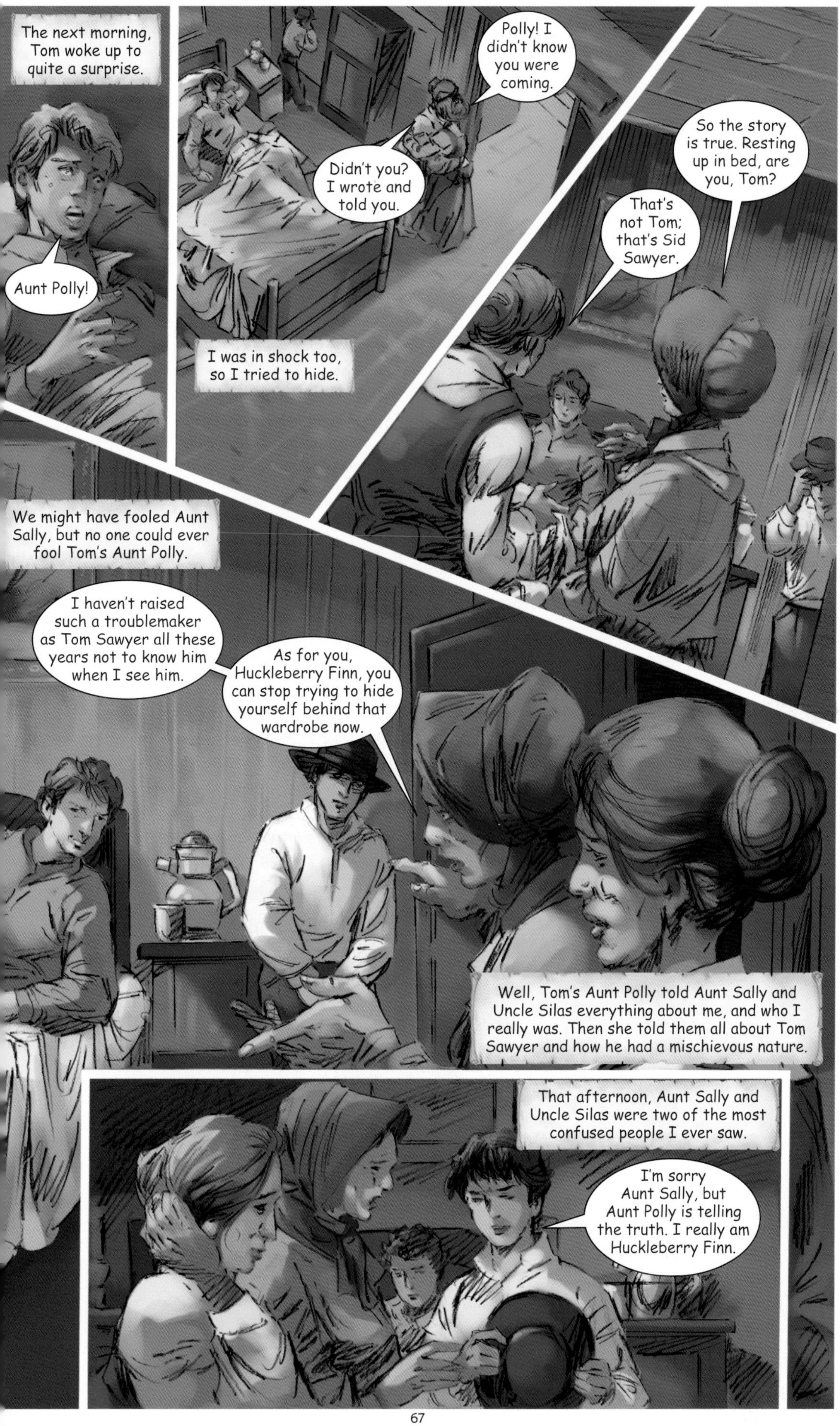

The next morning, Tom woke up to quite a surprise.
Aunt Polly!
Polly! I didn't know you were coming.
Didn't you? I wrote and told you.
I was in shock too, so I tried to hide.
So the story is true. Resting up in bed, are you, Tom?
That's not Tom; that's Sid Sawyer.
We might have fooled Aunt Sally, but no one could ever fool Tom's Aunt Polly.
I haven't raised such a troublemaker as Tom Sawyer all these years not to know him when I see him.
As for you, Huckleberry Finn, you can stop trying to hide yourself behind that wardrobe now.
Well, Tom's Aunt Polly told Aunt Sally and Uncle Silas everything about me, and who I really was. Then she told them all about Tom Sawyer and how he had a mischievous nature.
That afternoon, Aunt Sally and Uncle Silas were two of the most confused people I ever saw.
I'm sorry Aunt Sally, but Aunt Polly is telling the truth. I really am Huckleberry Finn.

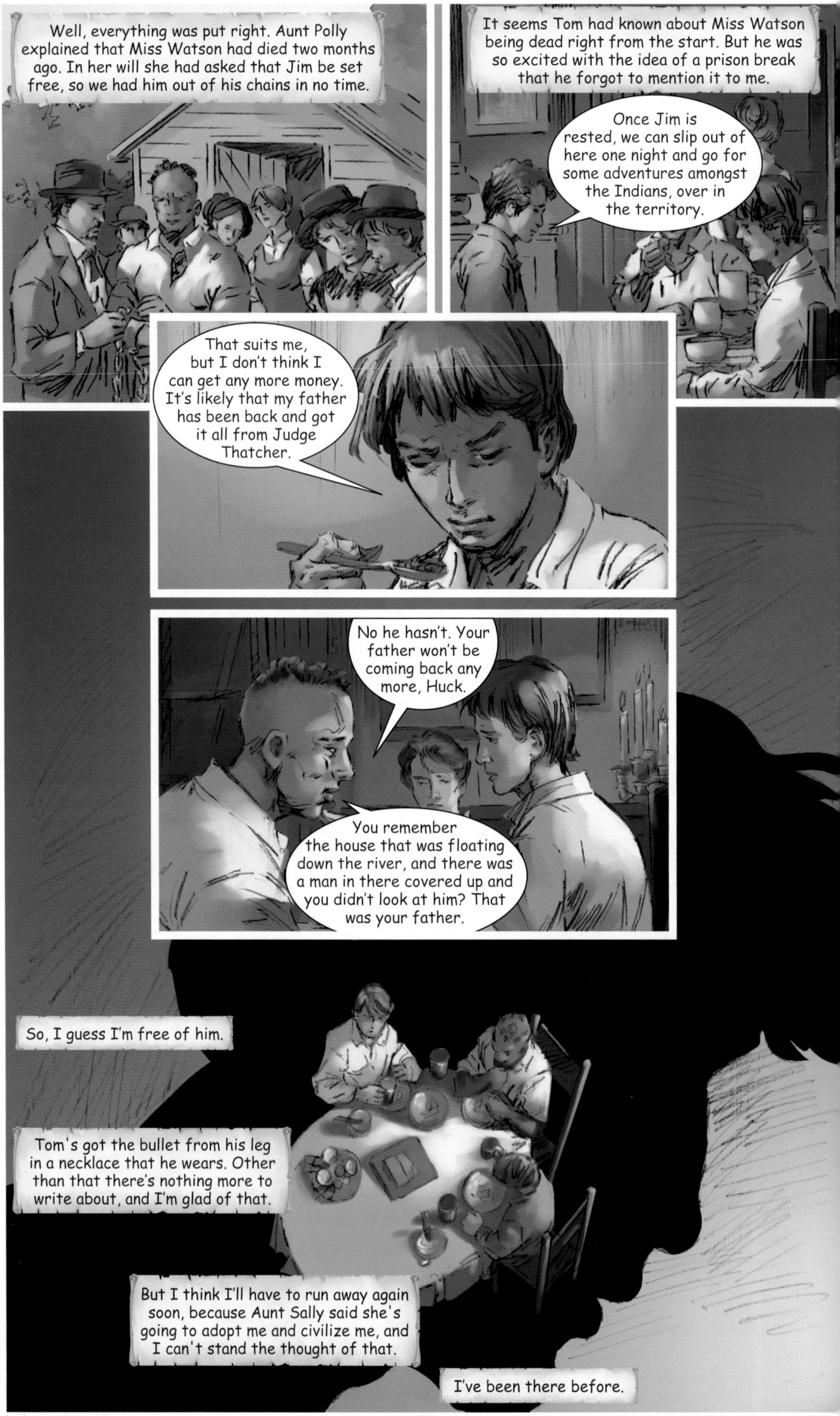

Well, everything was put right. Aunt Polly explained that Miss Watson had died two months ago. In her will she had asked that Jim be set free, so we had him out of his chains in no time.
It seems Tom had known about Miss Watson being dead right from the start. But he was so excited with the idea of a prison break that he forgot to mention it to me.
Once Jim is rested, we can slip out of here one night and go for some adventures amongst the Indians, over in the territory.
That suits me, but I don't think I can get any more money. It's likely that my father has been back and got it all from Judge Thatcher.
No he hasn't. Your father won't be coming back any more, Huck.
You remember the house that was floating down the river, and there was a man in there covered up and you didn't look at him? That was your father.
So, I guess I'm free of him.
Tom's got the bullet from his leg in a necklace that he wears. Other than that there's nothing more to write about, and I'm glad of that.
But I think I'll have to run away again soon, because Aunt Sally said she's going to adopt me and civilize me, and I can't stand the thought of that.
I've been there before.

Don't Miss Mark Twain's

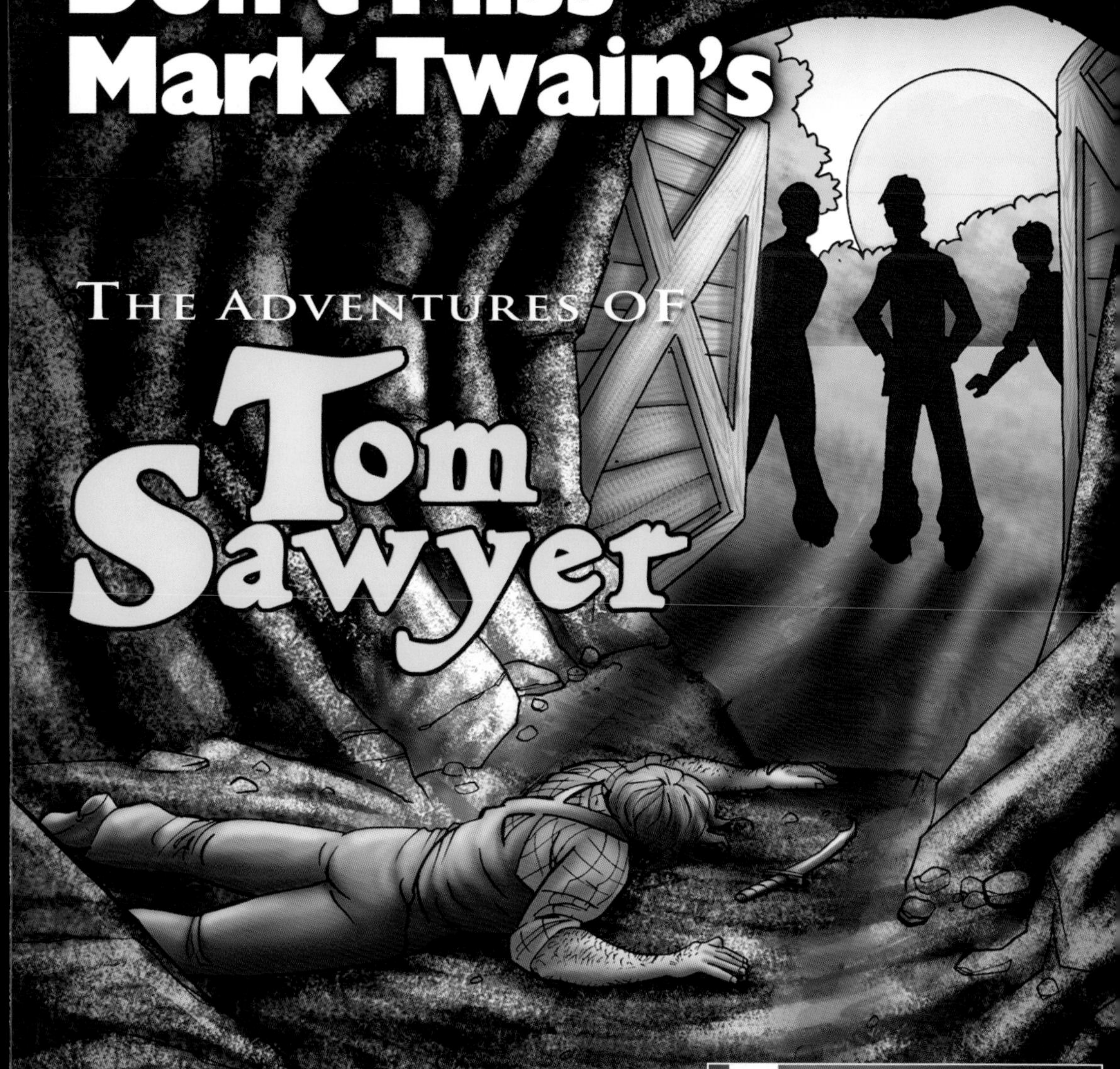

The Adventures of Tom Sawyer

Late one night young Tom Sawyer and his friend Huck Finn witness a terrible scene in a graveyard and are forced to flee from the scene. They swear never to reveal their secret to anyone and then find themselves entangled in a series of dangerous and thrilling adventures, with desperate men constantly at their heels. Have the boys got what it takes to become real-life heroes and will they ever be able to reclaim their normal, carefree lives ever again?

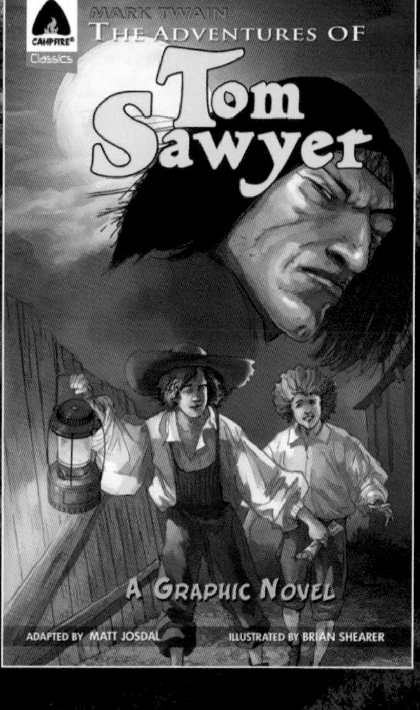
CAMPFIRE Classics
MARK TWAIN
THE ADVENTURES OF
Tom Sawyer
A GRAPHIC NOVEL
ADAPTED BY MATT JOSDAL
ILLUSTRATED BY BRIAN SHEARER

ONE OF THE GREATEST NOVELS EVER TO COME OUT OF THE UNITED STATES

SLAVERY In 19th Century AMERICA

Slavery in North America began in 1619. however, it continued right through until the 19th century, the period in which The Adventures of Huckleberry Finn is set.

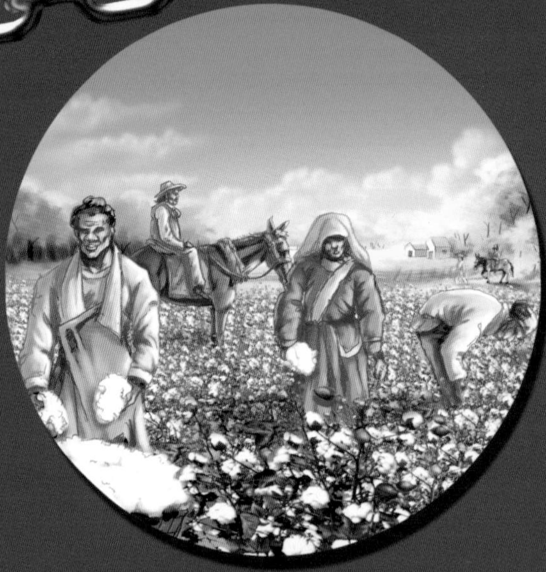

◀ COTTON PLANTATIONS

Huge cotton plantations sprung up in America during the late 18th and early 19th centuries. To pick, gin (remove seeds) and bale cotton, took a great deal of work. Africans were forcefully transported to these plantations to work as laborers, where they would work from dawn till dusk every day. They were often beaten and had to live in tiny cabins. Children were not excluded and were made to work because of their ability to pick cotton free of stems or dirt. They were also important workers because they did not have to stoop as low as adults and suffered less back pain from the constant bending.

Slave Driver

A slave driver was a slave specially selected by the master, who directly supervised the other slaves. He was in a position to punish them, so it was not surprising that he was often hated. However, if he was a compassionate man, he was also able to take care of the others.

▶ STEAMBOATS ON THE MISSISSIPPI

Winding its way through the heartland of America, the great Mississippi River was closely linked to slavery. Steamboats were a symbol of both bondage and freedom. They were used to transport slaves to various plantations, and acted as cargo ships for slave-produced commodities such as cotton, sugar and tobacco. They also provided the opportunity for the world of slavery to be left behind. Slaves often escaped, passing themselves off as passengers or workers, on these boats. In addition, they brought news of far-flung family and friends to the riverside slaves.

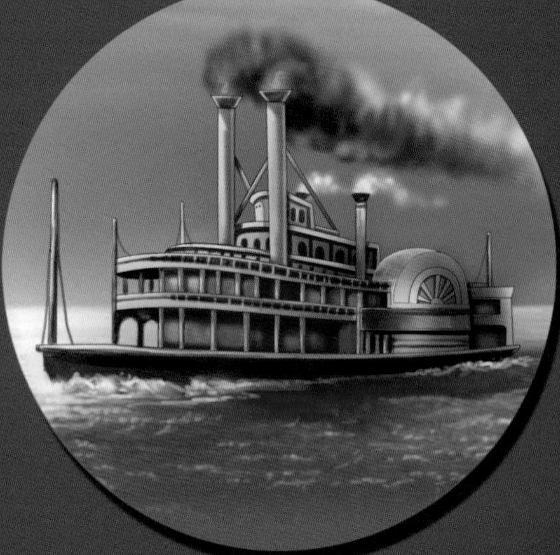

Life on the Mississippi

Mark Twain was a steamboat pilot in his younger days. He describes the Mississippi river and life as a pilot in great detail in his book, *Life on the Mississippi*.

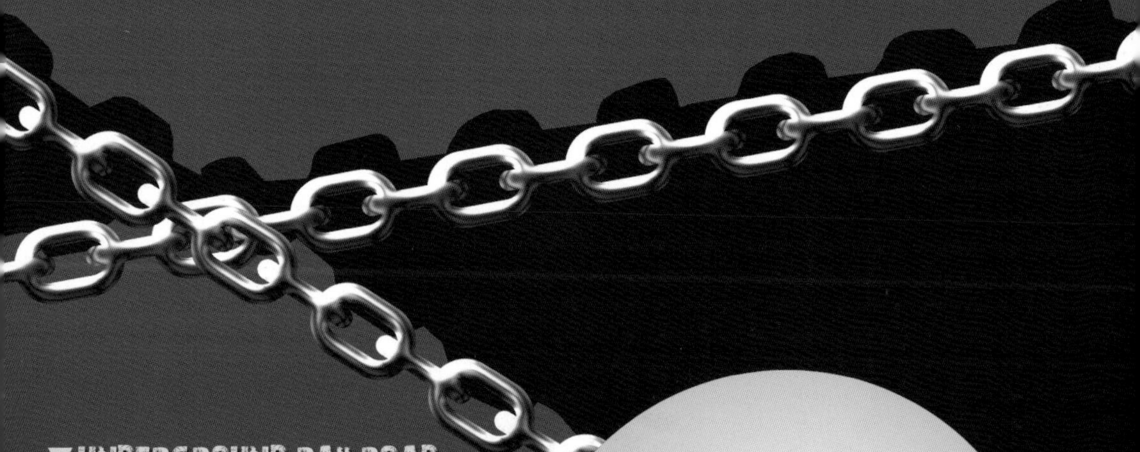

▼ UNDERGROUND RAILROAD

The Underground Railroad was not really a railroad but a network of secret routes used to help runaway slaves escape from the southern states and eventually into Canada and freedom. The slaves were secretly transported from house to house, until freedom was secured. The homes of people who helped the runaways were called 'stations'. 'Conductors' were the people responsible for moving the fugitives from one station to the next. By the middle of the 19th century, it was believed that more than 50,000 slaves had escaped using the Underground Railroad.

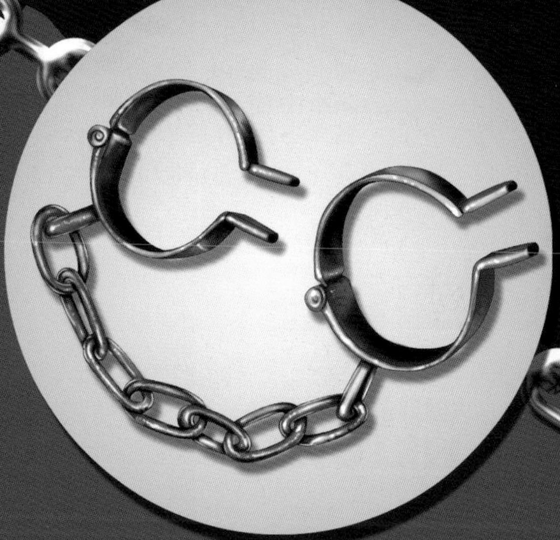

Moses of Her People

Harriet Tubman was a runaway slave who used the Underground Railroad to escape. She was known as the 'Moses of her People' after helping around 300 slaves reach freedom. She was such a threat to plantation owners that they offered a reward of $40,000 for her capture!

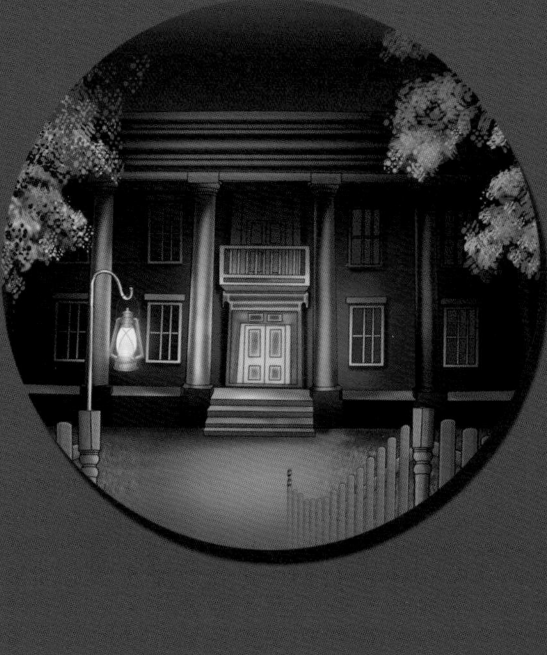

▲ ABOLITION OF SLAVERY

Abolitionists were people who wanted to end slavery in the U.S.A. In 1831, a newspaper called The Liberator was founded by one of these abolitionists, named William Lloyd Garrison. It called for immediate freedom for the slaves. The National Antislavery Society was also formed around the same time. The antislavery movement, however, caused bitterness between the northern states, which had abolished slavery by 1804, and the southern states, where slavery was firmly established. This, among other things, led to the Civil War (1861-65) in the U.S.A. In 1865, the Thirteenth Amendment to the Constitution officially abolished slavery once and for all.

Henry 'BOX' Brown

Henry 'Box' Brown was a slave who escaped from Virginia in a goods box in 1849! He squeezed himself into a crate and arranged for it to be shipped to a free state. The box traveled 350 miles by wagon, railroad, and steamboat. After the 27-hour-long journey, he emerged a free man in Philadelphia, and later became a famous abolitionist.

More Great Classics from Campfire

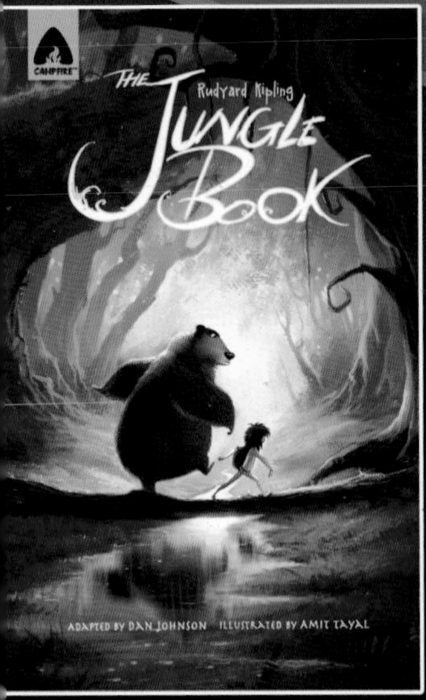
CAMPFIRE
The Jungle Book
Rudyard Kipling
ADAPTED BY DAN JOHNSON ILLUSTRATED BY AMIT TAYAL

The Jungle Book

The adventure of a lifetime begins on the night a man-cub called Mowgli, escapes certain doom at the hands of the tiger, Shere Khan. Raised by a wolf pack and taught how to survive by Bagheera, the black panther, and Baloo, the bear, Mowgli comes of age and soon the hunter becomes the hunted as the boy and tiger square off in an epic struggle to the death.

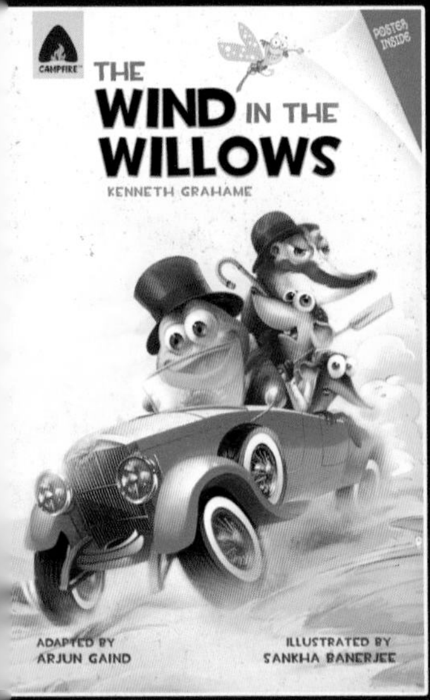
CAMPFIRE
POSTER INSIDE
THE WIND IN THE WILLOWS
KENNETH GRAHAME
ADAPTED BY ARJUN GAIND
ILLUSTRATED BY SANKHA BANERJEE

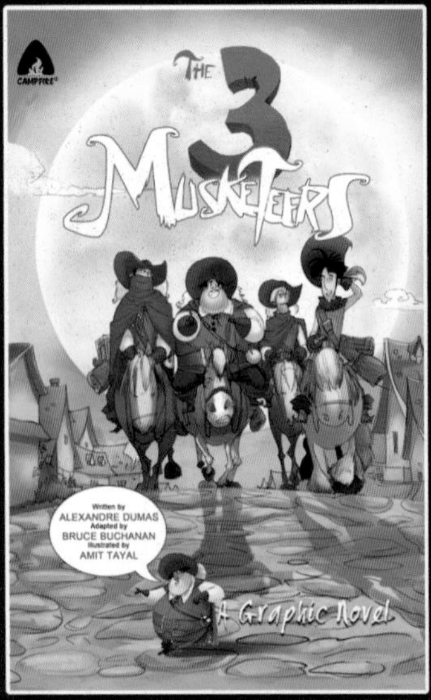
CAMPFIRE
The 3 Musketeers
Written by ALEXANDRE DUMAS Adapted by BRUCE BUCHANAN Illustrated by AMIT TAYAL
A Graphic Novel

The Wind in the Willows

Tired of spring cleaning, and in search of adventure, Mole heads down to the river where he makes friends with Ratty. After spending lazy days on the river they make the mistake of visiting the rich, exuberant and totally reckless Mr Toad. When Toad buys his first automobile, Ratty and Mole find themselves plunged into a dangerous adventure involving theft, a prison break and the siege of Toad Hall.

The Three Musketeers

Young d'Artagnan has only one ambition – to become a king's musketeer. With these dreams, he comes to Paris and befriends Athos, Porthos, and Aramis, the three musketeers and falls in love with Constance, Queen Anne's linen maid. Soon d'Artagnan and his friends find themselves fighting to foil the evil Count Richelieu's plot to disgrace the Queen.